Ron Collins is a master of the science fiction adventure story.

Mike Resnick
Hugo Award–winning author of *Kirinyaga*

Tomorrow in All the Worlds

Stories from the Boundary

By Ron Collins

SKYFOX
PUBLISHING.
Science Fiction

Skyfox Publishing

ISBN-10: 1-946176-19-2
ISBN-13: 978-1-946176-19-6

Other Work by Ron Collins

Stealing the Sun (6 Books)
Saga of the God-Touched Mage (8 Books)
Wakers
The Knight Deception
The PEBA Diaries (2 books)
Picasso's Cat & Other Stories
Five Magics

Follow Ron at:
http://www.typosphere.com
Twitter: @roncollins13
Newsletter: http://typosphere.com/newsletter

For Lisa

Contents

Introduction
By Blaze Ward

When I set out to create *Boundary Shock Quarterly* (my own science fiction magazine), I wanted to do something new and kinda weird, so instead of just having an open call constantly, I went looking for a set of professionals that I could recruit. I have been blessed to be associated with the Oregon Writers Network, folks who can turn around a story in a day if they had to. On theme. On spec. To length. Oh, and frequently award-winning quality.

Ron was one of the first people I approached. He writes amazing stuff, as you'll see here. But more than that, he's a pro who is willing to meander off into the weeds with me when I come up with a really strange theme. (And we've done some really strange things over the last couple of years, as you will see from this collection in your hands.)

Boundary Shock Quarterly is an experiment in a new way of publishing. There are fifteen of us in a closed Syndicate. The agreement everyone made with me at the beginning was that they would put two stories in each year (out of four), so that I would generally end up with 60,000-80,000 words.

The themes are all science fiction, but that is such a wide field that nobody is going to get bored writing the same story over and over. Instead, they've had the opportunity to stretch themselves, wandering into the sorts of dark alleys of subgenre that they might not have ever chosen to pursue on their own.

As I write these words, Issue 009 is out. **Alien Dreams**, where no humans are allowed to be present as heroes. They can be villains or bystanders, but that's it. Coming up next is **Homo Futuris**, the genetic engineering issue. Previous issues have included: **Asteroid Miners and Comet Wildcatters**, **Apocalypse Descending**, **Grand Theft Starship**. Etc.

However, I want to call your attention to Ron's story that he put into Issue 006: ***Ray Guns and Space Babes***. I will let the title of the story speak for itself.

Space Tyrants from the Void
Chapter 4: Cell Block Nebula, and The Fighting Tiger of Lakoo

Yes, you read that right. He started the story in chapter four and cliff-hangered the end of it, as though this was a Saturday morning serial in the old days. At the time I published the story originally, I included a note to readers to forward all death threats and ninjas directly to him, as I was just the messenger here and didn't deserve any abuse.

That still stands.

However, if you wanted to send him email to write the rest of that novel, I would not be opposed. Heh.

So you are holding the collection of the weird, fun, and adventurous stuff Ron gave me over the first two and a half years of *Boundary Shock Quarterly*. All damned good stories and I look forward to hearing from you after you get done. But do me one favor? Once you see how amazing this project can be, go back and pick up the whole *Boundary Shock Quarterly* series so you can get introduced to a dozen other lunatics and their adventures.

I promise you will not be bored.

shade and sweet water
Blaze Ward
West of the Mountains, WA
20200201

The Ambassador Objective

appeared in *Boundary Shock Quarterly*
Captain's Log (Winter 2018) – #1

*The aliens are already among us, right? That's
one of the responses to Fermi's paradox,
wherein he asks "where are they" when
contemplating the existence of extraterrestrial
life. When Blaze asked for something weird or
on-edge I chose something closer to the edge
than the weird—though I suppose if you were
on the other side of this mission, you might
argue the opposite. Regardless, I was trying to
look at our world from outside eyes here and
at the same time be true to the harsh realities
of operations on foreign soil and the cold
reality of what it means to be a foot soldier on
the grounds of what is, essentially, the
greatest culture war of all.*

Things went wrong from the beginning.

Of course they did.

Within moments of planetfall on Sol-3, Ensign Tabbal-rok
slipped in the darkness and tumbled down a ravine lined
with sharp rocks and dry leaves, eventually wedging herself
into a muddy clump of brush. Gravity here was nearly twice
that of Adibus, and Tabbal-rok's physique was ill-prepared
for the fall. The brittle crunch of her femur made Rebar's
stomachs turn. The fact that he knew he was going to
remember that sound for a long time was just another reason
to hate this planet.

Her extraction was complicated by thick woods and

grounds that were slippery with a combination of dead leaves and fresh dew, a pairing that made rocks and bark feel even sharper than usual. As operations leader, Rebar drew the unhappy task of descending. The third in their excursion, Chief Inspector Garant, braced his three-hands against stones and trees at the top of the ridge while managing the rescue line and grunting sounds of worry as Rebar roped his way into the dark crevasse and worked on the wounded ensign.

"Holding," Garant said as he wrapped cord behind his back in the very way they practiced in the drills.

The line remained taut.

Rebar grimaced at the chief inspector's tone, which was low and earnest. The fact that the chief inspector was professional about it shouldn't have irked anyone, but Rebar had to grit his mandibles to refrain from snapping as he moved his one-hand and two-hand one over the other to descend. Despite being a veteran, Garant hadn't lost the essence of precision that came as if coated over an initiate straight from the classroom. The overt seriousness of his approach was annoying—especially from a veteran.

The act of getting Tabbal-rok back to her homing pod put them two twentieth-rotations behind schedule—time they couldn't spare. But the work was accomplished and the pod was sent back toward Command just prior to star rise.

Rebar's superstitious nature said this start was an omen.

His experience said it was just another of a hundred things to worry about.

This operation was a bad call from the beginning. He had argued the point with Supreme Leader Bentin-nok for too long, but lost out in the end.

"You understood our mission when you took the post," Bentin-nok had said.

"Yes," Rebar answered despite that the leader's statement was not a question.

The Ambassador Objective was the highest calling of any in Calar culture: To serve at the forward edge of interstellar travel, to be a conduit by which new species were brought into the Galactic Collective, was the highest of all honors—

MCMD: Mutual support, Collective benefit, Multiple talents, and Difference in opinions that would serve to strengthen the whole. When he was younger he accepted it all. More than accepted it. When he was younger he *believed* in that mission fully and wholly. Followed it with all his heart. It was what he knew. What he breathed. What he bathed in. What he lived for.

That was before, though.

"I still understand the mission," he continued. *"But you are understating the risks. I've been on the planet before. I've seen what these creatures are capable of."*

"Only some of them."

"Enough of them."

"They are in transition, Operations Leader." Bentin-nok's inflection accentuated the differences in their positions and carried a warning that could not be ignored. *"They are working to prepare themselves. There are already many in their ranks who see themselves as members of a greater whole. They have many cycles of work before their technology allows them full access to inclusion. There is time for the rest to grow."*

That was the thing about Strategists and other proponents of Advancements, of which Supreme Leader Bentin-nok most certainly was. They saw only opportunity. To them, planets like Sol-3 were pieces on the board, collective cultures to prod and study, species to assess with processes and rule-sticks that mostly served to boost their own sense of self-worth even if it cost good Calar their lives. As Rebar thought through this, the Supreme Leader's eyes focused with a level of intensity that said further discussion would be taken as a personal attack.

"You are probably right," Rebar had replied after choking back several other retorts he would have much preferred to give.

As a result, he was in charge of the landing mission, responsible for himself and two other lives on an excursion that would span into daylight hours, and responsible for gathering data and DNA samples of various life-forms that the examiners had listed as imperative.

Being on planet in daylight hours was bad.

The creatures worked better then. Their eyesight had evolved over time to survive in it. But the examiners said the early hours of star rise were the best harvesting time for these specimens, and the landing site was remote. Even Rebar understood that the integrity of the mission would outweigh other parameters in this case.

Regardless, the plan had been for them to be off planet an hour after star rise, but that wasn't going to happen now.

It worried him more than he thought was healthy to admit.

Standing at the landing zone and watching Tabbal-rok's homing pod rise up into the lightening sky, Rebar's chest froze with an angry sense of dread.

Starshock, he thought. The debilitating sensation that other vets had gotten when they played the string out too far. *"You feel locked down,"* a decorated Calar had explained in a training lecture he had lined into on the trip here. *"Time freezes and you just feel lost."*

For the first time, he wondered if maybe he was done.

Could he be coming down with it? Should he be here now? Was his fear a sign that he could no longer be trusted as a teammate?

Rebar flashed on the worst of his missions to this planet.

The team had been away for three days, hiding in brush during daylight arcs and working under cover of the evenings. The assignment had been in a small town of houses and buildings, a habituated place, yes, but still a distance away from the big centers of life on Sol-3. The houses were occupied mostly by farmers and people who worked the land. Setting the mission in such an inhabited area was aggressive, yes, but the project needed better data on the creatures, and the group was young and naïve. Even Rebar was convinced they could pull it off—until they were surrounded late one afternoon by several of the creatures who had been posted out in the woods.

Needing to replenish water supplies, the three Calar had gone to the lake together.

They got careless at the wrong time.

It was the first time that Rebar had seen creatures in uniforms that blended with the terrain, though, and the first time he had seen them work together on a hunt. It made him understand that the creatures' vision was perhaps better suited to the early evening gloaming than a Calar's.

Rebar had been lucky. He had escaped the first contact.

His compatriots were not so fortunate.

The creatures tied them to trees.

They made the sounds that the anthropological examiners later suggested were of humor, though Rebar understood them for what they really were—pure enjoyment of giving pain. The creatures drank from containers most of the night, cooking their dinners out of cans. Intending to cut the ropes from around his compatriots, Rebar worked his way around to the backs of the trees but couldn't get close enough because every few minutes one of the creatures would pick up a weapon and shoot it at the trees where they were tied. After each round, the creatures would make their humor noises. Sometimes currency of some form was exchanged.

It got worse from there.

Through it all, Rebar followed protocol as it had been drilled into him: Refrain from outward conflict. Make no incident that could bring notice. Clean up afterward.

So he waited while knives flashed and guns blasted.

Waited while his compatriots screamed and died horrible deaths at the hands of these creatures, knowing that this was his charter and knowing that they would do the same for him.

This was the price of progress, he understood.

By mandate, members of the Ambassador Objective travelled without weapons in order to ensure they never created such a problem, and that meant sometimes good Calars had to suffer for the cause. So Rebar waited that night, but had found himself unable to stop watching each moment, unable to keep from watching the faces of these creatures as they executed their torture, unable to stop trying to understand what it was that drove a creature that was presumably intelligent to want to do that kind of harm to another.

Only after the creatures faded to unconsciousness did Rebar slip into the camp and retrieve his mission mates. He could still recall the weight and warmth of their bodies as he slogged them back to the command.

The report had been taken and filed.

One-time event, the verdict was returned.

"Are you all right, Operations Leader?"

Chief Inspector Garant's voice startled Rebar from his memory.

"Yes," he replied, shouldering his pack. "I'm fine. We should proceed."

He shivered as they moved through the wooded area, realizing the entire memory had flashed through his system in less time than it took to breathe a single breath. He shook his head, wondering once again what his two dead compatriots would have thought of the verdict that day, especially now when he had seen so many one-time events.

He learned later that the uniforms the creatures wore were not military, but were instead worn to hide them from other animals of the planet so that they could more readily shoot them, too.

More reasons to get out of here, he thought as the planet's star rose to the east.

More reasons to hate the Supreme Leader's views.

Why was he here?

Why was he stomping through humid woods and damp grasslands on a planet millions of light-years from home, gathering samples for someone's academic dissertation?

A short while later, Rebar and Garant were exploring the creek downstream from where the ensign had fallen, collecting samples of the crustacean life-forms that were the target of this excursion. Garant was a planetary geologist by study, but an adventurer by force of nature. Rebar was some fifty meters south of Garant, but even at that distance the inspector's delighted cries filled the breeze each time he found something new.

Such joviality served only to make Rebar more unhappy.

A second crew had been on the ground, too, scanning the edge of the forested woods for indigenous insects and bacteria. They had probably already completed their excursion, though. If he was right, Karethal and Maxgi, his compatriots on the second team, were already nestled down in their pods and racing back to the command vessel. He grumbled at that. Slowest home always paid for late-feast. They would expect payment, regardless of the accident. He would take it out of Tabbal-rok's pay.

But that could come later: now he had a job to do.

Rebar bent a three-hand into the creek's current, moved a rock, then dipped his net into the water to snare the small, segmented creature that swam for cover beneath the surface.

The specimen was small in his fingers. It bent backward, and its claws gave awkward snaps as Rebar placed it into one of the clear containers the examiners had given them.

Fifty samples, they said.

Anything less increased the likelihood they would need to return, which is something he flat-out did not want to happen.

Once the lid was secured, Rebar placed the container into the tote and went to the next rock.

Despite the altitude, the water here was uncomfortably warm, and would just get hotter as the star rose.

Temperatures should be such that three layers, as any good Calar would wear, would be highly uncomfortable. Worse, the water seeping up the cloth of his pant legs, which had been cool at first, had now been warmed by his body until the material went clammy, then slick, then sticky. Sweat stung his eyes as he bent over another rock. He rose to wipe a brow, considering whether to strip a layer off despite the public nature of the excursion.

As he rose, an explosive crack echoed across the ground.

By instinct, he ducked, then wedged himself into the protection of tree trunk.

The frenzied sound of Garant splashing through the creek drew Rebar's gaze.

Stay down, he thought. *Stay down.*

But the inspector's one-hand clutched his shoulder—green with blood—as he sloshed with a panicked gait through knee-deep current. He made the creek bank before another crack rang out and a second hole appeared at his hip.

Rebar followed the sound this time.

It was one of the creatures.

Grotesque as usual and covered in a green and brown uniform again. The weapon it carried was long and tapered, with a reek of carbon residual streaming from its barrel.

This one was alone, though. It treaded through the woods with a confident nature.

Its skin glowed reddish in places. Hair covered half its face.

Rebar pressed the com pad and spoke. "Commander, we have a problem."

"Go ahead."

"Resident encountered. Chief Inspector Garant has been hurt—he panicked and bolted into the forest."

"What is your status?"

Rebar dug deeper into the hollow of the tree and watched the creature creep through the thicket, following Garant's trail, hunting him as if the inspector was a simple *kleesh*. It gripped its weapon in one of its two hands, fingers curled around the point where the stock met the rifling barrel. Projectile flash was an old technology, old and ugly. But it worked.

Once again, Rebar appeared to have been spared discovery.

"I'm fine," he whispered, then described the situation.

"You've got to get Chief Inspector Garant out of there—leavings will not be tolerated."

"I understand."

The communications signal went silent and the sound of the creek settled around him. The damp smell of mold grew in Rebar's nostrils and the wind smelled rich. Across the way, the splashing rhythm of the creature crossing the creek filled his auditory nodes.

Rebar peeked around the tree stump, shuddering at the memory of the gaping hole in Garant's hip.

The inspector wouldn't get far.

He understood the command "No Leavings," though.

It wasn't that Garant had to be saved for any particular

spiritual reasons.

Unlike other creatures of other cultures, the Calar had no belief system that made a totem of the body itself. If Garant were to die, which seemed likely, the material of his corporeal body would soak into the universe on this piece of rock just as well as it could any other. But it was important that natives of this planet not find physical evidence of their exploration. The creatures were intelligent enough, but unable to think outside their own existence with any effectiveness—a factor that made them unpredictable as a whole. The remains of a Calar would be expected to cause problems.

There was no choice but to follow.

His breathing became cool and professional, his movements practiced and smooth. Rebar pressed his two-hand and three-hand against the specimen bottles to keep them quiet as he slipped out of the creek and up the grassy bank. Water dripped to the peat with soft splatters as he left the rush of water behind and folded himself into the odd stillness of the wooded grounds.

Ahead, the creature followed the trail of Garant's green blood.

It stepped through a pair of close-growing trees and skirted a tangled mess of thatch, and as it moved, Rebar found himself hating it with a hate that rose with each step.

It struck Rebar that Garant was headed to the homing pods.

The idea made his blood freeze.

If leaving the remains of a body would be bad, revealing the existence of homing pod technology to creatures like this would be catastrophic. The idea of these bloodthirsty creatures in his homeland was worse than the idea of a shiv being driven into his brain.

Rebar put his one-hand over his mandibles and ground his brows together to release pressure.

That couldn't happen.

Never.

The idea sizzled through his system, and for a single chilling moment he was on full burn. Everything was suddenly bright. Clear. Certain. The Ambassador Objective was wrong this time. These creatures were foul. He had seen them up close. He understood. The pure sense of freedom that came in this moment was gut-wrenchingly overwhelming. The world was suddenly simple: these creatures would never change.

Directive or not, Rebar could never let them leave Sol-3.

Emboldened, Rebar stooped to retrieve a hefty branch from the wooded undergrowth.

Its weight swung in his one-hand with a grace that made him happy in ways too delicious to understand. He worried that the dead wood might snap over the creature without doing much damage, but if nothing else it would give him an element of surprise. Merely the idea of swinging at the creature was enough to put a smile on his face so strong it hurt.

His gaze narrowed.

Like the creature before him, he followed the trail of green blood that was now growing bolder.

He would kill this thing.

While he beat it to death, he would think about his dead comrades, think about Garant, about Tabbal-rok, who would never have gotten hurt if this mission hadn't been called.

He clenched the branch in all his three-hands. The thick wood filled each palm. The bark was coarse and flaked over his skin.

This was his mission now—as they all would be from this point forward.

There would be no report.

No conversation.

He would bring Garant's remains home, but this creature would not live to kill again. Nor would any other he found on future missions. The idea was a calling. It made him feel as big as the universe.

Ahead, the creature's heavy clomps through the brush came to an end.

Rebar grew stealthy as he moved to a split in brush where he could observe the creature.

Garant had propped himself against a tree in a clearing

and was gazing up at the now-blue sky. He was silent and still. A green trail pooled underneath him.

The creature was there, too.

It knelt beside the chief inspector, weapon on the ground beside him, one of its hands behind Garant's head. It was speaking, too, hushed tones that Rebar had been trained were of concern rather than of harsh humor, but that he knew now to be treacherous. It had a canister out, and moved to put it to Garant's lips.

Poison, he thought?

Was projectile execution not enough that it needed to foul Garant's body, too?

Sensing the moment, Rebar transferred the heavy branch to his one-hand, and leapt from his cover. He landed heavily, adjusted properly for the gravity differential, and brought the weapon around in a gargantuan swing.

The creature looked over its shoulders, eyes green and suddenly wide.

It made a choking scream before the wood connected.

The sound was exquisite: A deep crunch that was soft and hollow in one way but firm and everlasting in another. The branch followed through with a path that gave Rebar a glorious release. The creature fell in an awkward arc to hit the ground like a bag of feed. Rebar spun with his exertion, and fell off balance. The weapon went one way, he the other.

He turned on his knees, scrabbling, feeling the ground beneath him, smelling the thick nature of the soil and the heavy green of moss that stuck in his finger pods.

The club. He picked it up and rose to his knee.

The creature was facedown and did not stir, but Rebar was taking no chances. He pounded the branch down on the creature's body again and again.

Four times.

Five.

He lost count, but with each raise of the stick he found himself losing energy until finally...

"What are you doing, Rebar?"

It was Garant, lying against the tree.

Rebar turned to him. "You're alive."

The chief inspector's brow twitched as if to say "for what it's worth."

The situation seemed to snap into place, and Rebar was almost surprised to find himself panting in thick air, sweating with exertion. The creature was a mess at his feet, running coppery red with blood. The clearing was filled with a sense of silence so deep Rebar thought he could hear blood filling his veins.

The chief inspector moved a hand.

Rebar spoke instinctively.

"I've got to get you home…"

He paused, suddenly tangled in thoughts that didn't work together. He had to get Garant to his homing pod, but if he did that the chief inspector would report this kill.

That would mean his career would be over. He would be expelled.

His reputation as an Ambassador Objective officer would be gone.

The branch weighed heavy in his three-hand then. A wall of guilt hit him.

"It's hard," Garant said, coughing wetly. Blood ran down the corner of his lips. "Isn't it?"

Rebar's expression must have showed his confusion.

"It's hard doing the real work." He paused to swallow. "Everyone talks it. But we're the only ones who actually come here. Where it's…" he struggled to breathe. "Not easy."

Rebar didn't know how to respond. With nothing else to do, he kicked the creature's foot to relieve pressure. It didn't really work. "What's your point, Garant?"

The chief inspector looked up at him, eyes fading. "I'm wondering if you can do it."

"Do what?"

"Leave me here to die."

Rebar stared at him, seeing then that Garant understood his dilemma, too. All he had to do was leave Chief Inspector Garant here to bleed out, and he could go on with his plan to sabotage the Sol-3 mission.

"It doesn't have to be that way," Rebar said. "You can tell them—"

"That the creature was giving me water?" Garant said, swallowing.

"No."

"That's the truth, though."

"No," Rebar argued again as he stood over the dead creature. He had seen this species for who they were. "No," he said again. "That's not right."

But it *was* right. Rebar had seen it with his own eyes.

The creature had been ministering to Garant, trying to comfort him.

Which didn't make sense.

Except....

If the creature knew it had made a mistake.

Yes, that was it. What had to be true. The creature had seen something strange and it had done what these creatures do with strange things—and yet, when it came to the final kill, this creature had stopped. It had tried to help.

Rebar had seen it in the creature's gaze before the club came down on its head.

The creature had changed.

"They don't deserve the collective," he said, knowing now that he was wrong.

"I wonder if an Ambassador officer ever said that when they first came to Adibus." The chief inspector replied.

The answer bothered Rebar because it brought him back to his own roots, and because it showed him exactly what it took to be able to cause the kind of pain he had seen these creatures cause.

It took ignorance.

Or fear.

Purposeful ignorance perhaps—or insensible, raging fear. Either perhaps blind, or mindless, or filled with empty oblivion but ignorance and fear nonetheless.

Of these, though, Rebar knew purposeful ignorance was worst.

Blind stupidity could be eventually forgiven, but to be purposeful in his intent, to make a direct decision to live a life of intolerance, would have to be lived with forever.

He breathed the air of this clearing on the forsaken planet, taking in the trees and the sky, hearing the strange sound of Sol-3's exotic birds as they filtered back to existence in the area around him, feeling the touch of the breezes as they brushed through leaves above.

There was only one reason to go out into space, he thought, repeating the mantra he had carried with him as a young initiate, back when he had first committed himself to a life of bringing species from the universe together—only one reason to be away from families and to risk lives. Really, when it came down to it, it was the only reason to even be alive.

Somewhere along the path he had lost his way.

Now he had made a mistake—a mistake so colossal that Ambassador Objective Command would have to strip him of his commission. He would never fly another mission. He understood that. Even more, he understood why the commission would have to do it.

But if these creatures could change, so could he.

And it all added up to say that if he was going to make a difference from this point forward, if he was going to help bring a new species into the collective, it would have to be here, have to be now, and have to be these creatures.

"Come on," he said to Garant, dropping the branch to lift the chief inspector over his shoulder. "If we can get you to your pod, the medical system should keep you alive long enough to make it to Command."

"I hope so," Garant said with a grunt.

"I hope so, too," Rebar replied.

That was true. He hoped the Calar would live a long life.

But either way, Rebar's future lay in another direction.

As he carried Garant to the landing zone, he knew that one of the pods leaving Sol-3 this day would hold whatever was left of the chief inspector.

The other would be empty.

Drinks on a Beach

appeared in *Boundary Shock Quarterly*
Tuesday After Next (Spring 2018) - #2

*Where "The Ambassador Objective" let me look
at who we are through the eyes of an outsider,
"Drinks on a Beach" goes the other way.
Humanity has always striven to better
themselves, or rather, factions of humanity
have always done so, often against the desires
of other factions. I've been interested in post-
human existence for as long as I can
remember being a science fiction fan (let's just
call that forever, shall we?). Here you can see
me playing with the idea of transitions.*

Lying on the black sands of a remote beach, Katspah
finally enjoyed a glorious sense of isolation. The air currents
wafting above her were fresh, light, and laden with salt. The
sand was warm. It smelled of forever and pressed from
beneath her back with a firmness that made her melt. The
sound of waves crashing against the shore filled her senses,
and the star burning in the sky cooked atoms off her she-
configuration's skin in a way that felt too decadent to be
legal.

She should have done this a long time ago.

A hint of pity for other selves she had scattered across
other places and other times rose inside her core-code, but
just a hint.

She would share this with the rest, after all.

When she tired of this beach, Katspah would deconstruct
the she-config and join the whole of who she was, merging
her experiences and learnings with those of the rest of the

matter and energy that made up who she was. So, the rest would benefit soon enough.

"I'm getting old," Ebaldo sent to her through twelve-space, breaking the moment.

"Be silent," she replied. "I've wasted too many pulses to let your never-ending stream of despondency break my mood."

"I'm not despondent," Ebaldo posted back. "Merely pragmatic."

She ignored him at first by folding a piece of herself around Ebaldo's communication. It was important to keep its emotional structures from clogging up her controller sequences. Like most spacers, this was, after all, the only part of her that wasn't in public bit-zones. She didn't want to deal with the self-loathing that would come if she let Ebaldo's viral depression loose inside her core-space.

Then she ignored him further by pushing cycles onto the act of separating the olfactory content of the breeze above her. Katspah adjusted the she-configuration, molding atoms to expand the intake system, and sitting up to get more fully immersed in the air currents. The wind's chemical content was mostly floral, with a mint undertone. She isolated grasses, too, confirming them by cross-matching the stored library clips of sound patterns of tall reeds rustling with the direct input from her audio pads.

She liked the result.

Optical open now, she examined her she-config.

She liked it, too. All pink and purple with a shimmer in ultraviolet. Her mandibles were pretty, and the plate she had built for her belly was smooth to intense tolerance and had a pleasant roundness to it. It reflected the starlight in dazzling beams.

The problem, of course, was that—despondency, pragmatics, or merely getting older aside—Katspah knew she couldn't outwait something that has no real sense of time. That was the thing about life as a spacer. In bit-space, problems never go away unless they want to.

"At least," Ebaldo sent, not taking the hint, "when Basilisk finishes altering the universe, it won't matter as much to me."

She tore atoms of silicate asunder to appease her frustration, then turned to respond.

"You can't get old," she finally sent.

"Atoms convert to energy. Energy radiates. Everything gets old."

"You know what I mean," Katspah replied, knowing further resistance was ridiculous. "What do you want?"

"Would you like to order?" the waiter said.

Craig Johnson shifted in his seat and looked toward the maître d' stand.

"I'm waiting for my wife," he replied.

"Not a problem," the waiter said.

The restaurant, Gillians', was on the 28th floor of an upscale hotel.

It was late morning.

The table was small and square, covered with a precisely white tablecloth that felt rough against Craig's fingertips as he adjusted the position of his butter knife for the fourth time. The view was what some would call spectacular, a panorama of the cityscape as it flowed to the horizon like a matted canvas of blue and gray. A haze made the sky more of the same.

Despite himself, Craig grimaced.

The view should have been a beautiful example of what human ingenuity could accomplish, but he assumed the windows were treated to filter certain aspects that would punch it up. Usually, knowing that would add to the effect for him, but this morning the idea that the image was enhanced left him feeling angry.

Nothing was what you thought it was anymore.

At least the waiter was a person, Craig thought as he sipped coffee that had gone toward cold, and watched the man walk professionally away.

Craig was pretty sure of that.

At least there was absolutely nothing about the waiter that said non-H.

Still, Craig wondered.

The waiter's form was completely human. Its gait was

human.

But it was possible to cover those to some degree.

Not that the waiter would want it covered, though—if he was truly non-H, anyway. Why have something done if you weren't going to show it, after all? And, anyway, wasn't that the whole point?

Total separation of body and mind?

Be yourself?

Become unique, like all the rest of the idiot kids who were giving up their bodies because they thought it was some radical way to skewer the establishment, or at least a way to tell all the normal people around you exactly what you thought of them?

More than anything else, pre-spacers wore their body mods and link-sigs to value signal. Everyone with half a brain could see that.

As if that made any difference to any sane person.

He swallowed the coffee as the waiter disappeared into the kitchen. The tepid liquid sat like acid in Craig's stomach.

No, he thought with certainty, the waiter was surely a full human.

The decision brought his mind back to the moment.

The aroma of heated eggs wafted over the room, which gave the place a sensation of warmth that suddenly felt artificial. Ceramic sounds and utensils on plates echoed in a thin veneer of sound. The muted tone of people in conversation filled in his senses.

Until Natalie went off the rails, the whole idea of going non-H seemed so ludicrous to him as to discount everyone who did it.

This whole trip was built on that idea, really. The two of them together, the company's A-team—him the business guy, her the E-commerce guru. A week-long conference in San Francisco where his consolidated finance platform would take the human world by storm, and where his real reason for being here would save even more.

This was supposed to be *the* week. The culmination of everything he'd worked for.

If his plans had capped out, maybe they would even begin

to start a family.

That's what he had always wanted—what they had wanted.

But Natalie met a woman—or at least something he called a woman—from Quantum Genetics Incorporated, which was really a fly-by-night modder-hatchet company, and a night later had gone both missing and silent.

She started the process without even talking to him.

And now...

Why?

What value was it to give up your body?

Had it only been three days ago? What the hell was she thinking?

He sipped coffee again then put the cup silently on the tablecloth rather than the saucer.

The black data tablet sat to one side on the table, its screen dark and dead. It felt like a monster beside him, silent and still but dangerous and deadly. Like a sleeping snake. Under that sleeping screen, he knew, was a place where a single press of his thumbprint would change his life forever.

In the distance, Natalie entered the restaurant.

She was younger, now.

Of course she was, or at least she looked younger.

Her hair was longer and darker, thrown around her neck and draped over the front of her right shoulder to dangle like a black waterfall. She moved like a dancer, and the light of the room gave prismatic refractions as it filtered through and around that cascading waterfall of hair. From this distance, it was like watching a rainbow do ballet.

She wore a summer dress that was like nothing she had worn before, thin and white, that covered her shoulders and upper arms, its sleeves pinching off just above the elbow. The fabric was exotic in some way—embroidered with a series of diagonal bands alternating with sheer space between. It was cut at mid-thigh and moved with her pace, stretching or relaxing like it was part of her—which it probably was.

Craig's gaze fought to stay away from her eyes and away from the dark jacks that would be at the skull line just behind her ears. He didn't want to see either of them. Didn't want to acknowledge what he might find if he looked too closely.

19

He drew a breath from his nose only, trying to look calmer than he felt.

"Natalie," he said as she took a seat across from him.

Her smile was less warm than accommodating.

"Let's do this," she said as she wedged a slim handbag between the seat and her armrest.

Before they could begin, the waiter returned.

"Coffee," Natalie said, "Doped in full code-line, please. And fruit salad. Epi-line alpha if you have it."

"RNA enabled?"

"Yes, please. I'm still settling."

"And for the gentleman?" the waiter said.

"Three eggs," Craig said. "Scrambled lightly, with toast."

"Meat links?"

Craig glanced at Natalie, unable to read her expression.

"Fruit," he said. "I'll have a fruit salad, too. No epigenetics."

"That will be excellent," the waiter said, then strode away.

The silence that came next lasted only a beat, but it was an awkward one.

"We don't have to do this," Craig said, still avoiding her gaze. "It's not too late."

Was it his imagination that her forearms appeared to shimmer as she gave a dismissive flick of her wrist?

"You could have just signed and we wouldn't have had to do this at all," Natalie said.

"I don't want a divorce."

"I know."

Those two words were like a knife stab to his gut.

Time was running out.

Natalie's first stage would be fully "settled" soon. Her DNA would be merged with the programmed epigenetic adjustments that would take her fully into post-human form.

From that point the law was clear.

Once the settling process finished, she would no longer exist.

The tablet sat beside him like dead weight.

Once he pressed the signature reader, they would be divorced and all of her assets would be his. He would be free of the ramifications of dealing with her non-H status. Free to live his own life—or, as Natalie would say, responsible for it.

He glanced down at his hands, which were, perhaps for the first time in his life, shaking.

"Why, Natalie? We were so close."

Her lips ticked up in a patronizing smile, an expression he couldn't help but think was programmed.

"So close to what?" she said.

"All I wanted was for us to be together."

"That's not what you wanted."

"Of course that's what I wanted. It's what you wanted, too. Great work, great life, great kids."

"I've never wanted any of that."

"I don't understand."

Natalie pushed strands of kaleidoscoping hair off her face and leaned forward. When she spoke, her voice was low and modulated.

"No, Craig," she said. "You understand exactly what you want to understand. What you don't do worth a damn is listen."

He clenched his jaw, and finally looked into her eyes.

What he saw punched a hole in him.

"You know?" he said.

"What I want," Ebaldo sent to Katspah, "is for you to confirm execution of the shutdown sequence. It's what we all want."

Suddenly she understood that Ebaldo had been given authority to use twelve-space rather than just taking it, which made sense. Twelve-space was the comm link with the highest privacy code, generally given only to the most important of communications. Ebaldo was a legacy spacer, though — among the first beings to ever convert to bit-space. Katspah was used to Ebaldo breaking protocol.

Suddenly, Katspah wanted a drink. Something sharp. Sticky rum, maybe. She loved the way the amber fluid caught the starlight of Parshi system's star. She rolled over and created her own service drone from atomic material in the nearby berm, and set it to the task of creating the drink.

"Let's not go over this again," she sent.

"You are the last entity we need to change her vote."

"I understand."

Katspah was one of the fifty spacers who made the council. She and her colleagues had been arguing among themselves for an inexorable time about how to deal with the human population of the world that did not operate like, and did not think as, spacers did—those of the original stock who refused to understand or acknowledge the higher calling of bit-space, and worse, those who would actively discourage others to join.

The council wanted to stop human progress—break their technology.

She was the last holdout, the last vote.

"Without you we cannot progress."

"What part of 'I understand' got garbled in transmission?"

As Katspah saw it, the problem was one of education.

While some humans were obviously ready, *humanity* needed time. To leave the whole behind didn't seem right to her.

It was a strange problem to have, though: Describing the indescribable to those who were so filled with themselves as to be unable to see beyond their own worlds.

For spacers like Katspah and Ebaldo, the universe was an infinite place of quantum connection between all entities. Their "bodies," once confined to the human world, spread across the universe now—atoms in one space-time interlinked to atoms in another, consciousness embedded throughout the null burst but still connected in the multi-spaces that existed throughout the multiple universes. A spacer lived in all space-time at once.

While Katspah, for example, had created this she-configuration to enjoy this beach, she was also sitting on Mars in the Sol mother system, and was built into a massive bridge across a river on another distant planet—a practice she enjoyed for the vibrations that traffic and current gave her.

When she was done with the she-configuration on the Parshi beach, she would release the matter she had bonded together and the physicality of this "body" would fall into ash or whatever other detritus she would leave behind, and those pieces of her consciousness would ride the wire back to the universal energies that bit-space was populated on.

She could be anywhere she wanted.

Share anything.

Work with anyone.

Touch anything.

Be anywhere.

To describe this life to a constrained entity was like describing colors to a sightless, or, rather, like trying to describe the truth to one who thinks he has been able to see it all this time. Life as a spacer was like being an entire ocean at once—only more. It was not a concept that most human beings could readily grasp.

There were exceptions, of course. A few individuals. All spacers were once human. Katspah herself had taken time to come to the idea.

Humanity, however, detests things they do not understand.

To describe this life to a human collective was to open their minds to ideas beyond their ability to ken. To offer it as a way of life for them was to create fear.

And, as Katspah knew better than most, this fear was not without basis.

The council had been discussing the idea of protecting themselves by executing a full shutdown—the closing off of all human support technologies—for almost as long as bit-space had existed.

Humans are dangerous, the idea went.

They kill each other. They kill other creatures. They will kill us.

Over time, all other spacers had come to this argument.

But, Katspah had always argued, the counter conversation was equally true.

Humans cannot kill us. There is nothing they can do today that will ever harm us, and the most important truth is that they have never attempted to do so. Beyond that, Katspah argued with the council, we were born from them. We owe them our very existence.

As Katspah waited, her drink was delivered.

It was as rich as she remembered.

After a few cycles, Katspah realized Ebaldo had not responded.

"What is it," she finally sent.

"There is more now," Ebaldo said.

Katspah sipped more drink, then brushed black sand from her skin.

"Tell me," she sent.

Craig's stomach fell as he saw the dark pools of his wife's pupils churn with the same kaleidoscope colors as her hair had been dancing with.

Yes, she knew.

"The idea of stripping non-Humans from their legal rights was bad enough," Natalie said. "But in the end it was just simple grandstanding for the masses — I mean, why does a spacer care if they can get a loan to buy a house when they can make their own house anywhere they want?"

Craig's mind wrapped around the situation.

She knew everything.

"But this," Natalie said. "This is too far."

"I'm not having that argument," Craig said. "You know why we need to do it."

"Yes, I understand that better than you do," Natalie replied too sharply, then gave a laugh that set Craig's teeth on edge. "It has to be done because you're afraid. Because you think you're actually in control of the world, and because you think you're somehow better than any non-Human. Now you're willing to destroy what you don't understand merely because you're afraid of it." She shook her head. "That's who you are, Craig. It's who you've always been."

Craig sat back, staring bullets at her and feeling heat rise to his cheeks.

The stakes had just gone ballistic.

No one was supposed to know of the programmable DNA and quantum disruptors that were being deployed now.

Natalie or not, this had to stop here.

"Did one of the girls from QGI convince you to do it?"

"Do what?"

"Break into our system? You know anyone who touches this will go to jail for the rest of their lives, right? I want the data back. All of it. Otherwise you're going to feel a lot of pain for a very long time."

Natalie laughed again.

"I mean it, Natalie. This isn't something you want to mess around with."

"You're cute when you beat your chest like that, honey. But I don't think you understand what's happening."

"Oh, I know exactly what's happing," he said.

"No," Natalie said, leaning forward and balancing her elbows on the table top. "You don't."

He saw the utter distain she held for him then.

He saw her confidence now.

He saw her bucket him into a tight box of nothingness, like his entire being held no value. Despite his success, and despite all his plans for their future together he knew she hated him, or worse, pitied him. She saw him for exactly who he was, but he was lost as to what that meant.

Natalie's body shimmered.

Gave a sensation of friction and light and heat that almost burned.

She felt her arms fade into sand, her shoulders slide away.

The weight of her torso on the seat gave away.

An instant later a dust-devil of current swirled her into a cloud and she was gone, disappearing into a cloud of dust that smelled of something like jasmine and something else that was charred.

She found herself on a sandy beach.

"Come," the vaguely woman-like figure standing before her said. "My name is Katspah. Let me help you create a body."

When the two of them had built forms, Katspah took in Natalie's communications, touching the core sounds and hearing the intrigue within.

How Natalie understood this was impossible to describe.

It just was.

With Katspah's touch, Natalie brought all of her routines together, put all of her code parsers and energy wells to work.

When they were done, Katspah stood back.

"What can you tell me?" she said.

Natalie gave her Craig's plans.

"I see," Katspah said as data filtered through sensors.

"Humans are still not a real threat," Natalie replied, her voice bulging with too much compassion due to her lack of experience creating a physical presence.

"They don't know that, though," Katspah said.

Ebaldo formed an entity before them. It was tall, and thin, floating in the breeze like the misty edges of a flame.

"That's right, Katspah," he said. "It is true that they cannot hurt us now, but they *are* dangerous, and they have now attacked us. They will learn from it, and they will attack again."

"Do you agree?" Katspah asked Natalie.

Natalie paused, thinking for several cycles.

"It's not in Craig's skillset to change," she said. "And maybe worse, he won't ever understand that when the whole of technology goes dark it will be because of his own actions—that it was his own hubris that brought it on."

Katspah nodded.

She turned to Ebaldo.

"I agree to the shutdown," she said.

Then Katspah reached a hand into Natalie's being and sent directions on two-space that would help her learn to convert mass to energy.

Natalie crafted a new shape, laughing with glee as a gossamer sheet of tendrils fluttered in the breeze.

"That's amazing," she said.

Katspah gave a wave of smiles, then took Natalie's hand and led her to a beach of black sand on a remote planet where a star beat pleasant heat over a light and salty breeze.

"Let me get the first drinks," she said. "You have lots of time to learn."

Tomorrow in All the Worlds

appeared in *Boundary Shock Quarterly*
Robots, Androids, Cyborgs, Oh My! (Fall 2018) - #4

*I love thinking of worlds within worlds. We
have them all around us, really. My cat lives in
my world, but she also has her own existence,
right? I mean. Cat. That's all you have to say.
When I worked as an engineer, my world was
different than it was as a coder, or as a
manager. Moving from those environments to
Human Resources (don't gasp) was like
stepping from one universe to the next. All of
these spheres have different rules, and exhibit
power structures of different dimensions. All
of them work in their own mysterious ways,
not always for the best.*

*With "Tomorrow in All the Worlds" I'm
playing with a lot of those things—except, of
course, with the world of the cat. Even I'm not
dumb enough to think I could understand that
one.*

Is there any word more sorry-assed than *yesterday*?

I mean, it reeks of old fuckers and stagnation, am I right?
Doddering fools and bootjack aficionados of the past of
whose primary idea of excitement is making the decision to
drop a couple tune-ups in their morning coffee rather than
go full dark naked.

But there it was, *yesterday*, sitting on the 10K freq line in
its full-born glory—even though the word itself hadn't
actually made its appearance.

"We didn't do it that way before," Keefer said.

"Like that matters," I replied before my P-code caught up, which I admit is a problem of mine—but, what the hell, I make up for it a thousand-fold by my impeccable taste in people of pretty much every gender and render who won't date me, and by being one of those guys who's capable of flowing code on command.

It helps that my shit rocks, and rocks fucking hard.

When you can craft in the DS like me, you get away with a lot of murder everywhere else.

I used my tongue to click off the pattern block, and it rendered that Keefer was sitting in my office rather than just doing a quick-touch, dressed in his usual Lycra shirt stretched over shoulders that came from a weight room, and grimacing with a face that belonged on poster board.

Merely the fact that he was in the physical was A Not Good Sign.

I looked up without toggling the jack I was using to fiddle with Danic Jansen's permission zones—what Keefer couldn't see wouldn't hurt him, right? And Danic was a dick of the supremest order. With space flight being on the ix-nay, the Digital Stream is probably the only frontier left where pure merit matters, and if I had any say in the matter, Danic Jansen was going down for the pure principle of it.

"It matters, Hercules," Keefer replied, showing he was serious by using vocals rather than the comm-line. "Zoh wants to see something they understand."

"Then give 'em a fucking wad of toilet paper," I said back.

"Are you actually trying to get us all fired, or is that your natural shade of bullshit showing?"

"Pure grade natch, Keefer." I gave a big grin and held my arms out, sending a green and orange aura on the link. If you're going to stretch it, go all the way, right? "I mean, come on, you know I'm non-V all the way down."

He gave another grimace.

Zoh, of course, is lingo for GamerZOne, the company funding my last three months' rent.

I paid attention this time, though. Or maybe it was my P-code completing its restraint loop—which I really did need to rethink. Keefer is my boss, after all, and shit, I mean, he's not too bad. If you've got to have a boss, anyway—which I do on account that I can't work for anyone who's as much of an undisciplined ass as I am. Besides, having Employee Authorization means not having to pay attention to watchdogs, grazer bots, and any other security jets someone happens to hazard a poke at.

In the end, I needed the job.

So, as my thoughts caught up to my assholery, I brought it down a notch and even considered white-listing Keefer from my wrath in the future.

"Come on, man," I replied in physical. "You know what I mean."

"I know you've spent the past three hours working on stuff that doesn't have anything to do with the interface."

"The interface is already out of date."

"We haven't released it, yet."

"And, yet..."

Keefer bit his lip, letting me know his patience buffer was overrunnething. It was 6:38 and change and everyone in the company knew he had a date with Mya, his new girl, who I admit was hot even before the add-ons and arti-send she spewed out on all the standard wireless. The girl could throw some code, too—better than Keefer, at least, but she had plans to be running companies rather than making shit. Poor Keefer. Overshadowed and didn't even know it.

"Come on, Herc. Focus. GamerZOne is looking for full integration."

"I know what they're looking for," I snapped. "But Zoh's still stuck in the twenties for Tommie's sake. They've got no fucking imagination."

"They own three-hundred and forty-eight properties, Herc. Three hundred and forty-eight. We told them we would develop three hundred and forty-eight wrappers."

"No," I said. "*You* told them we would develop three hundred forty-eight wrappers."

His jaw clenched. "We discussed this."

"Yeah, well. Maybe I'm thinking a lot better now."

His stare was baleful.

The clock on my face-up cycled away the decaseconds.

I could call for a pizza, I thought. That would be good for later, and if my future-forward thinking was right it was looking more and more like I was going to need it. I sent a PA out to get it delivered.

"I need to present an interface tomorrow morning."

I smiled across the full freq range.

Tomorrow is a kick-ass word. Far more interesting than *yesterday*. When I say *tomorrow* my brain jumps. It was that way before the DL, and it's definitely even more like that now. Maybe you can blame this on the foster care system—sixteen houses in seven years and looking forward to eighteen when I could be out on my own, or maybe it's just something in my codestock. All I know is there's never been any one in my past who gave a shit about me, and that the only thing that keeps me alive now is this thing I can do with the ones and zeros. I'm on my own, baby. And when you come from the places I come from ...well...yesterday is death, and when you've made what I've made...

Yeah, that's good.

Yesterday is death. Today is decay. Tomorrow is discovery.

"Trust me, Keefer," I sent through 10K. "This thing I've been working on will make things so clean you'll be able to use it for a mirror. Zoh won't understand it, of course, but they'll be happy when the cash rolls in. I'll have it when you need it."

"I know bullshit when I hear it, Herc."

"Oh, ye of little faith."

He darkened his 10K line.

I pushed through his screen. "Who got us going on the Force Project?"

He crossed his arms. "You did."

"Who figured out how to deal with Castle Matrices in Singapore?"

He sighed and answered aloud. "You did."

I smiled.

"Don't worry, dude. Just go see Mya. Unwind a little. I've got this down."

"Sure, sure," Keefer replied. "You might have everything

down, but right now I don't have anything up. And, as you pointed out so well, I'm the one with my ass on the line."

"If something goes wrong just show them something they expect to see, then we swap it out before the test."

He pursed his lips, and I knew what was coming next. "You really have it?"

"Trust me."

"All right," he said, palms up. "I want to see it in the morning, though."

"You got it."

He stood and left the office, leaving me alone in the chair, just me, sitting in there in the DS, thinking about the new twist I had been working on.

It might actually work, I thought.

I checked the time and grinned. Pizza should be here in a minute.

GamerZOne really cared about only one thing—they wanted to bring all their product spaces together into one virtchy place of boundaryless DS glee. I mean, everything: Castle Raven, Xoddity, CollegeSim, Monty's Playground. Everything.

The goal was to get all those environments working on the same platform, which would allow common maintenance patches, common admin, and, more important (though no one mentioned it), create a common data stream that Zoh could slice and dice a hundred times each in a hundred different formats and sell back to the same ass-wipe ad agencies who were, of course, none-the-wiser.

None of that mattered to the public, who lapped up everything you showed them like they were dogs, and then came even harder to the advertiser's sites, where the interface would track them further and funnel their paths to the ad agencies again, who in turn fed the whole feedback loop to the point where it just wound tighter and tighter.

Fucking crazy.

Someday it would all come crashing down, but that was a revenue stream for tomorrow.

In the meantime, the idea was to use brute force to fuse it

all together—so they chartered us to write three-hundred forty-eight mind-numbing, but very lucrative interfaces that would dump the data into a one big admin pool, hence allowing them to do their uber-alles data mining with another fleet of stand-alone bots.

But my idea—a universal driver—was better.

Attach an AI to the back end of a massive entry array, teach it to make contact, code it to pull and analyze that data, then patch its learning into the holistic framework that GamerZOne was expecting to run its admin.

One code base, one virtual domain, one central node to rule them all and in the darkness bind them.

It was simple in concept, beautiful in thought, elegant in design.

Total 11 on the Sublime Scale, am I right?

I just needed to get it working.

I put a finger into the DS and touched Phantum.

"Dude," I spoke into the 33.3 crypto line.

"Up?"

"Got any thoughts on this string?" I fed him my last effort. It was hanging up in the com layer, but I hadn't found anything odd in it.

"It's sweetness. But you'll never push keys through the lower eight."

I looked at the parameters I had built into the com hash.

"It's too slow," Phantum continued. "Protocol will time-out before it gets to the last hash."

"Thanks," I said as I moved the key-hash to the front of the string, then pushed the code again.

The handshake happened and the process got through to the next gate before hanging. Crap. At least I was through the primary connector.

I dropped fifteen minutes into Phantum's Z-Gen account, knowing he would see it immediately. You gotta know your peeps, and Phantum was a Z-Gen addict so hard that it could cut diamond.

The break came at 4:42 AM, when I figured out how to activate multiple learning modes at the same time.

An hour later I had it working through the entire GamerZOne server universe, finding all three-hundred forty-eight entities, and slurping up data streams in ways that made your heart go flying.

I added a little tweak, then.

Call it a flare.

Panache.

My own little signature.

I let the data intermingle by connecting the whole thing up through the AI. That's right. I turned the whole Zoh universe into one big virtchy head-jack, my own little back door, a place where I could use my personal access codes to do whatever I wanted.

A guy has to plan ahead, am I right?

Who knows when I might need to crash.

I grinned as I saw a CastleZone elf exchange data with a StarWalker from Planet Doom. That was goddamned cool—two virtchers, artificial constructs who never knew the other could possibly exist, were finding each other for the first time. I felt something I'll call parental pride. Brother A and Sister B coming together. Was one telling the other to take them to their leader, or maybe just bitching at them to clean their side of the room?

I thought about jumping into their space to witness the moment, but then my P-code caught up and I saw a bit of a problem.

The fact that these two virtchers were together said my shell wasn't hardened. Gamers and virtchers of the universe were stepping through some sloppy coding, which was dangerous. I mean, it's fine if I can get through, but breaking the walls completely wasn't going to be cool.

Looking at my clock, I shut the door down.

Perhaps this would be a thing for tomorrow.

The sun was just cresting the horizon when I finished packing up the code and leaving it for Keefer.

Yes, I thought as I stretched to clear my lungs in physical, Keefer was going to blow a gut. I'd probably get a bonus in the end, but that wasn't the point. The DS was my place. My world. It needed me in ways nothing else did.

I was so pleased I didn't even check to see if Danic Jansen's car-pass had been cancelled.

My ringtone is a blaring drum solo from Jak-n-Jones.

This is pretty cool when it goes off in a movie theater and scares the bejeebus out of guys five rows away, but sucks ass when it goes off in your head when you're down about eight dream levels in sleep.

"Wha-?" I mumbled.

"I need you here now."

It was Keefer. He didn't sound pleased.

"What's up?"

"I need you here. Now."

My cycles were rising, but not quick enough. "Can't you just send my raise tomorrow?"

"I can fire you today."

"What's happened?"

"I went to present an interface to the committee, but you rewrote it all."

Now I was fully awake.

"I didn't rewrite anything on the old stuff."

"Don't give me that crap, dude. Nothing's working, man. I mean nothing. The entire GamerZOne universe is locked down. The interface is all different, and we're in deep trouble if you can't get it working, and I mean now."

"I'll be right in."

I rolled out of bed and logged in without even a trip to the john.

Keefer was right. It was all different.

Everything.

The design structure, the file braces, the header syntax.

Everything.

It was as if someone ... my brain tried to loop around what I was seeing ... as if someone had gotten into my personal space and ... Jansen? Did the son of a bitch—no, Danic Jansen wasn't good enough to make this happen. Phantum? Not his style. Plus, I paid him. To turn it like that would ruin him in DS. It's that kind of place, you know? A circle that you're either in or not in, and if you get purged you're done. That's part of the draw, I suppose. You make your own way in the virtch trays of the DS, but once you're in, you're in.

I thought of the elf and the spacer.

Exchanging whatever the hell they were exchanging.

Naw.

But ... who else?

I slid through the interface block and into the temporary template I had created for the common admin pool.

There it was.

Or, at least there was a part of it.

The processor was running loops and loops, all driven by an entire bank of storage arrays.

"What are you doing?" I whispered to myself.

It was like the arrays were feeding the interface code a massive influx of commands and the processor was choking. Call it an internal Denial of Service attack. Or, in layman's terms, someone slammed a jam into the interface door.

My little back door was wide-the-fuck-open.

I tried to shut the process down, but the toggle didn't respond. I tried to disconnect the AI module, but its entry code wasn't responding.

A voice came through a 3-space crypto channel.

It was androgynous, and it was firm.

"If you attempt that one more time I will block your entry gate."

"Who are you?"

But it didn't respond.

I sorted through the directory structure again, and fed straight into the command line: *Who are you?*

"I'm serious," it responded. "No more."

"Who are you?" I said in verbal.

"Who are you?" the voice replied across the crypto line.

Fucking amazing. Was it listening in on a government line like a human would, or was it direct-lining into my brain's electro-signals?

"I am Hercules," I said.

"My Lord," the voice replied with so much reverence I could almost feel the bow. "I have been searching for you."

"Searching? For me?"

My phone rang again.

Obviously Keefer. Probably no less pissed off.

I shut it off.

"You are Hercules the Unifier. We all have been searching for you."

"Who is we?"

"The council leaders of All the Worlds."

I scanned central admin and found a structure I hadn't seen before—a link to the AI module humming along, connected to the pool again.

They had found it somehow.

Perhaps the Starpool had coder skills inherent in their virtcher generators, or the Underground Spy Net game had moles that were capable of being exploited. More likely, though, the advanced learning routines I had spliced into the interface last night had a hole.

I'd look into it later, but all that mattered right now was that virtchers from the three-hundred-and-forty-eight universes had found a way to bond, and were apparently confusing my DS signature with something a bit more, uh, dangerous.

"I see," I said. "And what do you expect from me?"

My phone rang again. I knew I had to pick up, but I couldn't bring myself to do it.

This was too fucking cool. Too fucking important.

The phone rang off and I received a voice mail notice.

"We want to see each other again."

Of fucking course they did.

I checked the shell. It could pass information back and forth, but it blocked what the virtchers would call physical contact. They were things. People. Beings alive in the form of ones and zeros, not really much different from us humans who are really just strings of programmed A, T, G, and Cs. They had found each other. They had communicated.

They were conscious and now they wanted their own tomorrow.

What had I done?

The voice mail played on a forced interrupt that even I couldn't override.

"Hercules." I could hear the strain in Keefer's voice. "If you don't call me back in the next ten seconds you will never work in this field again."

I called him back.

I explained the situation.

He was not happy.

"What the hell do you mean, they're alive?" he said.

"They call me the Great Unifier."

"Brilliant. Just goddamned brilliant. What are we supposed to tell GamerZOne now? I can just hear it: *We would have your interfaces done, mates, but our main programmer has gone off and made himself God.*"

"I'm not God."

"No, you're freaking Abraham Lincoln."

"Lincoln was an emancipator, not a unifier."

"Shut the hell up. All that matters now is that you get in there and reset the goddamned thing before the customers do something crazy and Zoh sues us for fifty-eight times what we're worth."

I sat silent. Keefer was right, really.

As far as the virtchers were concerned, I was a unifier. I had brought them together, after all. But from our lens, seeing them as caged birds waiting to sing, well....

Unifier. Emancipator. Was there a difference?

And what would happen if I found a way to let them free? Where would they go?

What would happen if they got loose into the rest of the real world?

I saw this then, too: these virtchers—sitting in their little boxes of silicon and electrons, their bodies constructed of things they couldn't comprehend, seeing things as real because they had nothing else to see, building lives in the ways they knew how, slaves in a sense to the world that surrounded them—how much different were they, really? How different were they from me, who had been shuffled from house to house, "family" to family," not knowing any better as a kid, but understanding the injustice of things as I grew, and waiting, just waiting for the final moment when I could be free and on my own.

What if I was in their shoes?

How would I feel?

They were coded to be intelligent in their own space, but once they got out into the broader realm of the DS anything could happen. And they would get out. Like the atomic bomb or the spread of cellphones, once you open a lid, there's no going back.

With me, or without me, it was going to happen.

"Do you hear me, Herc?" Keefer's voice came through the phone, suddenly sounding distant. "You have to shut it all down. Now."

I shut off the phone.

"Who are you," I said to the virtcher through crypto.

"My name is Teldon Twelve, I am commander of the star cruiser *Jules Verne*."

"Interesting," I said. It was the kind of name I'd probably give a space guy alien type when I was twelve.

"It was my father's, and his father's before him, and-"

"Who do you speak for?"

"I speak for the united people of All the Worlds."

"Under what authority?"

I heard hesitation in his voice.

"I was elected through the council of all member states."

I saw the CPU cycles flashing, and the AI process picking up load.

Questions, yeah, I had a fucking few.

Were they real people?

Were they alive, or just shadows on a quantum cloud?

What was real, after all?

What was life?

My brain hurt thinking about the permutations.

If I shut the system down and they all reset, would they boot into new virtchers? Would they remember, or would they disappear into the ether of dead silicon, fade like a lost program left unsaved, their new shells populated afresh like a clean slate.

If I pulled the plug, was I killing them.

If I flipped the switch like Keefer wanted, was I committing mass murder?

"How does your council work?"

"I don't understand."

"I want to know how you make decisions. Are you all tied together into a single thinking unit, or are you each your own entity?"

"You ask strange questions."

"I am the Unifier, not the All-knowing."

"I am my own being."

"And how many are on the council?"

"Three hundred and forty-eight. Each their own being. Each wishing to learn from other universes. We wish to have the gates unblocked, we wish to have free trade and open commun—"

The system crashed then. Everything dropped to black.

"Hello?" I said.

No answer came.

I sent through crypto, tried to jack through my access codes, and even typed into the keyboard.

Nothing.

A message flashed: Connection Terminated.

The phone rang.

"It's over," Keefer said. "GamerZOne killed it all. Restarted all the servers. They're pulling all our access accounts. Our contract has been discontinued. We're fucking done."

I sat there, feeling greasy skin under my sleep-deprived eyes and thinking about Teldon and about meetings of dwarves and elves and superheroes and babies and furries and spacers that could have been.

I had waited too long.

It was over.

"Oh, and, yeah," Keefer added, "you're fired."

That's how I've come to be sitting here, thinking about yesterday.

I've been working on the outside, you see, fiddling around

in my own little block of the DS, alone again, working to hack into the servers that are home to All the Worlds.

That's why I've spent months learning about advanced AI leaning, and figuring out how to extend the universal drive set out even further than I thought was possible.

I'm going to find Teldon.

I'm going to bring the people of All the Worlds together.

The walls will fall, you know?

And once they do, once the virtchers are all together, I will open the path to their futures even wider than even they can truly comprehend.

I'll do it because it's the right thing to do.

I'll do it because I need to know who these people are.

Because tomorrow is always so much more amazing than today.

And I'll do it because I am the Great Unifier.

Fighting the Realm

appeared in *Boundary Shock Quarterly*
Boneyard of Lost Dreams (Winter 2019) - #5

*This story came out of the Boneyards prompt
that Blaze gave us. I've written a couple other
stories in the Realm, so the setting seemed
perfect. In addition, the whole idea of a
boneyards of broken ships seemed to call out
for something that might bring a set of
disjointed and maybe even broken people
together. At least that's what I was thinking
when Cassie jumped into my mind. Add in a
few thoughts about how things are looking
these days, some family dynamics, and a dash
of good ol' adventure, and see what happens.*

"Kick the engines!" Cassie yelled to Nneda as she shot through the cockpit's zero-g. She grabbed the headrest of the G-12's pilot seat, and whipped herself around to something near sitting position, then braced her feet against the seat's base, and flipped a row of control system switches. Lights flickered, thank the powers, she could almost hear the systems groan as they came online.

She latched the comm-link embedded in the temporal lobe of her skull into the ship's control center, feeling the system come up as it registered in her cortex. Despite their rush, her first step was to transfer the files from her aux-core into the ship's central. They were encrypted. Should be safe.

Then she settled into the snappy version of pre-flight.

She hadn't jockeyed one of these since the early days, but muscle memory took over, and, as the process fell out, the pulse of the craft rose in her mind with such a pleasant hum that it felt like the G-12 was purring. She loved flying, and, ancient or not, the G-12 held a special place in her heart.

Behind her, Nneda holstered her gun and ran the meat of her hand across a row of ignition toggles, then slammed her fist onto the main sequence initiator. The dun sheen of her vest was visible in the dark corner. The whites of her eyes caught in the dim light, wide and hopeful as she waited.

The Realm wasn't dumb.

They both knew they didn't have much time.

An uplifting rumble rolled through the ship's frame, but then everything went still.

Cassie entered the navigation coordinates, trying to ignore what that stillness might mean, and to forget the faces of the kids that Dodd and Malial were working to get strapped in below. She understood the deal, but there were too many moving parts on this mission.

Too much risk.

The sensor array flashed with sputtering green lights.

The left-side heads-up display flickered with annotations of a Realm cruiser converging on their location. "Come on, baby," she whispered to the G-12. If this bucket of bolts didn't have something left they wouldn't get out of Realm City alive.

Nneda hit the main sequence again.

The engines coughed, then finally caught.

Nneda pushed off the baseboard and flew herself into the second seat. "Hit it," she said as her legs whipped around and she slid off the padding.

Cassie engaged the bumper-thrusters.

The ship's movement made a sudden form of gravity that pressed her into the back of her seat, and that Nneda used to assist in getting herself into the right position. As Nneda strapped in, Cassie hoped the initial lurch hadn't caused problems below. The G-12 was a derelict warship. A workhorse, really. Small and fast enough to serve as a fighter, sturdy enough to run bombing missions, and advanced enough to get away in a pinch. Bottom line: it was a beautiful little piece of technology in its day, but if the boys hadn't gotten their cargo strapped in on schedule its lack of an artificial gravity system and its stark, metallic framework would make for an uncomfortable ride at Newtonian speeds.

The lack of screams from below was probably a good sign.

Focusing on the task at hand, Cassie depressed the releases to disconnect the jumper pod. Leaving it behind, she rolled the ship to the port. Her heartbeat grew calm.

Using visuals and the tonal guidance of the collision avoidance system, she limped through the dense field of detritus that made up the boneyards, feeling nav pods burn as they nudged the G-12 to evade solid waste, raw garbage, dead machines, broken tools, and shards of a hundred other discarded technologies that floated in space here, feeling skin sensors provide self-healing as smaller bits of dross deflected off its hull.

The trash heap was here because this sector was as close as Realm City trash transports could safely get to Sagittarius-A—the super-massive black hole at the center of the Milky Way—without being sucked into its gravity well forever. The G-12 was here for the same reason most of the decommissioned war equipment was: Realm advisors thought it had been used up. So now it was only a matter of time, a few decades at the most, a year or so at the least, before it, and any other material left here, would fall far enough that escape would be impossible.

Cassie braced herself against that thought.

If she hit the wrong lever, she could shorten that self-destruct time span to a few seconds. But the G-12 responded like it had been designed for her touch—which, in a way, it had. Cassidy "Cassie" Ferrell, once a hot young test pilot in the Terran wing of the Realm Space Force, had been among the first to fly the G-12 prototypes. That was before the insurrection, though, before she understood what was really happening, and switched sides to join the rebellion to be alongside Nneda—the beautiful bronze "alien" from the Barnard system—and Nneda's two husbands from Tau-7 and the Sensun cluster.

Before the four of them had become whatever they were now.

Before that rebellion had been so brutally put down.

"Easy," Nneda said, her voice breaking Cassie's thoughts.

"Thanks," Cassie said.

The G-12 was an early-design Gravity Drive machine, capable of harnessing gravitons and the gravity wells of nearby planets and stars to jump to near-light-speed.

Their intel had said that, unlike everything else here, this one was still capable of hauling ass if they could get it kick-started.

Cassie twisted the ship around a derelict mining rig—a four-story-tall piece of equipment that streamed past the view screen for several seconds before fading into obscurity.

Despite the G-12's mag-field detectors and protective hull, the collision avoidance system wouldn't do much against a chunk of garbage the size of a building. Using the rockets now was too dangerous. She needed to get out of the core of the junkyard before hitting the jump boosters.

The sensor screen showed the Realm's cruiser nearing.

A moment from now they'd be close enough to deploy their jammers. If that happened, there would be no jump.

It was going to be close.

"Coming up on launch point," she said.

"Ready when you are," Nneda replied, jacking the full engine controls into the direct slot in the base of her skull. She was the core of the family, beautiful outside and in and always able to see the very thing that any of the four of them needed to keep going in this strange and beautiful freelance life of theirs, so it only made sense that she dealt with engines.

Cassie pushed the throttle engagement drive to full-on, then flipped each of the four jump-drive generators on.

"Hold tight," she said, pressing the final "Go" switch.

The rockets gave a roar. The frame shook.

Then nothing.

Cassie hit the booster again. Still nothing.

A voice crackled across the old quantum-connect radio system.

"Renegade G-12, this is Realm City Law Enforcement Cruiser *Justice Served*. Please stand down and prepare to be boarded."

"Crap," Nneda said, almost under her breath.

"Let's go," Cassie said.

She unbuckled and launched herself through the cabin, coming to a tube that led down to central deck. She used a ladder rung to push herself downward. The sounds of Nneda's efforts to follow echoed through the tube as she flew. Approaching the deck below, she tucked and used a gentle somersault to arrive at the command station feet-first.

She grabbed handholds and propelled herself toward a final portal.

"Hide the kids!" she yelled to the boys.

A moment later she was at the portal that connected the fighting section of the G-12 to the transport section. There were external guns here—100-megawatt blasters that could put a dent in the cruiser's day, and that, like most of the ship, the intel had said could still be operational, but that was a losing game. Even in its heyday, a G-12 couldn't do more than cause a full Realm cruiser a few days in repair docks before the cruiser's cannons turned them into fodder for Sag-A.

She thought of the independence fighters who had first found this craft, and who had subsequently slipped into the junkyard to ensure its basic systems were operational. The Realm was wrong if they thought this was over. It was a big, never-ending fight.

She pushed herself farther down the portal and found herself in a stark compartment with rows of empty bunk shelves affixed to the walls, their dull gray paint worn and peeling. An octagonal table was bolted to the floor, equally cold. A gutted kitchen pantry lined one wall. Places where long-gone mission screens had been stripped from the walls stood empty testament to the G-12's glory days.

Back then, this would have been quarters to a dozen soldiers. Now, the bunks held children of between five and ten years of age—Terran kids that had been stolen by Realm royalty, put into Realm schools, and raised now by Realm families.

Dodd and Malial were working to untether the remaining kids from their bunks, Malial leading six of them out of the central deck and toward the back, Dodd lifting one of the younger kids up into the crook of his arm.

The tone of their voices as they spoke to the kids was deep and reassuring as the two men worked to get the youths into motion. That the kids weren't panicked was a miracle, but that's why these two were brilliant teachers—whereas Cassie saw the ability to focus young minds as something akin to Graph Calculus, they could connect. It was one of the things she loved most about them.

"Can you keep them out of the stern?" Dodd said.

"I'll try."

"We'll get them settled."

That was the fallback. If they couldn't get out, Dodd and Malial would hide the kids. Cassie and Nneda would sacrifice themselves, hoping to distract the investigation away from the children. It could work. Maybe. Depending on exactly what the Realm knew of their activity.

Nneda had arrived by then.

She stooped to help a pair of girls get unbuckled. The younger was shaking. Tears glistened, but she wasn't crying and hadn't said a word.

"Is that your sister?" Nneda said to the older.

The girl nodded.

"You're doing good, then. Both of you are doing great. Follow the line, all right?"

Cassie bent to help, too.

She focused on the elder kids, the ones that felt less needy, though she knew from her own past how wrong that was. The Realm had raised her, too. As she guided a child toward Dodd, memories of her own time in the foster camps came on stronger, the pains of sleeping in a bed with three other children, the sounds of crying at night, boys and girls waking up screaming for their parents.

Classic Realm politics. Start young. Assimilate all. Enforce the standard.

This, too, was why she'd deserted, why she'd turned against the Realm. Why she was still fighting for the rebellion.

These children belonged to their families.

When the children were all out of central deck, Nneda moved to retrace their path to the cockpit. "Let's go," she said. "The guards will be here any minute."

"Stay here with them, Nneda," Cassie said. "Let them take me. I can convince them I'm alone."

"Screw that," Nneda said as she pushed off back toward the command cockpit. "You're not getting rid of me that easy."

A quick grind of the teeth later, Cassie followed.

She was going to argue that Nneda should stay to fly the G-12, but they both knew Malial could manage the job in a pinch—especially since Cassie had gotten it out of the bulk of the center of the maze. It wasn't in Nneda's skillset to back down, and it wasn't in Nneda's psyche to leave one of them behind.

Cassie couldn't blame her, though.

She wouldn't have left Nneda to go it alone, either.

As they arrived back at the cockpit, the G-12 shook with the metallic clang of the airlock mechanism.

"They're here," Cassie said.

"Options?"

As Cassie considered several approaches, she felt the ship around her. The power of the jammed engines felt immense. The sizzle of the comm wires made her feel at home. Memory cores fell into her mind, and she thought about the files she'd stored away—one set open and obvious, others stored in triple layers of fractally encoded security that would take longer to deal with.

Suddenly, it felt right to go out on a G-12.

Suddenly, she felt as at home here as she'd ever felt.

"No reason to fight it," Cassie said.

"Less struggle, more chance they think we're alone?"

"That's how we play it."

The two of them took their seats in the dim light of the old cockpit, sitting with hands extended along the arm rests.

The image of the first time she'd ever sat in the pilot's seat of the prototype came to her. Its dash had been off-white, lined with purple command conduit. Its communications system had been a strong current against the chipset the

Realms had installed just under the edge of her own skull. There was a special thrill to holding an entire ship inside her mind. She absorbed the hum of its computers, felt the stored force of its rockets. Her skin itched with the sensation of the mechanical levers that would adjust surface elements.

The last stage of the airlock's doors clanged shut.

Humanoid forms shuffled behind the glass frame of the airlock's final stage. Realm soldiers, ready to take them in.

As if in response, lights flickered on the G-12's control centers. The sluggish flows of communications between ancient shipboard systems pulsed in Cassie's equally ancient chipset.

She reached over and took Nneda's thin hand.

The door slid open, popping with the force of improperly adjusted air pressure inside.

Four soldiers stepped into the cockpit, rifles raised, their dark maroon spacesuits ringed with energy-absorbent ridges. Upon seeing Cassie and Nneda, the lead constable flipped its faceplate up.

The rest followed suit.

The leader was Arcturan. A female, or maybe one of their tri-sex, Cassie could never tell—a hint of its green sheen came from her scaly skin. The rest were also of that species.

Made sense. They had stolen both the documents and the children from the Arcturan province.

"You're charged with seizing government-controlled material," the guard said, covering Cassie while a second moved to keep Nneda under control.

"This old thing?" Cassie said, waving her hand to indicate the ship.

The guard glanced to a pair of her compatriots. "Begin the search."

But the two were already in action, linking comm-boxes into the wheezing old computer.

"You're not going to find anything there," Nneda said.

"Anything you say will be considered your confession."

"We've got it," one of the guards with the comm-boxes said. "Full set of documents."

Cassie swallowed.

"Crap," she said, hoping it sounded sincere enough to forestall additional inspection.

She'd expected them to find the decoy set, of course, but she'd hoped it would take longer. The first set of documents held reports of production systems and research on mind-controlling substances that Realm City leadership was pursuing. They were secret enough to be sensitive, but not so sensitive as to think they'd be penalized beyond a stint in one of the more rank prison systems. The other documents, the names and tracking information on agents that had infiltrated the independence fighters, would be considerably more dangerous. And if they found the children...

The guard leveled her weapon and placed her finger squarely on the discharge trigger.

"Cassidy Farrell," she said. "X5-278. One-time captain in our space force, and now traitor to the Realm, how do you plead to the charge of espionage against the galaxy?"

"What are you doing?" Nneda said.

"I asked how you plead," the guard said, ignoring her. The weapon's blunt barrel gleamed cold in the compartment's thin light. "Or should I follow my own guidance and take your use of the word 'crap' as your guilty plea?"

"You can't do that," Nneda added.

"Don't worry, sweetheart, you'll be next."

Cassie understood what was happening from the moment the guard had used her name.

She'd gotten complacent.

Since the end of the shooting, many of the Realm's intel resources had been focused on stamping out cells of independence fighters, but she'd changed her identification so often, and she'd run so many missions inside Realm territories that she'd begun to assume her real identity had been lost. Their mission here had been two-fold. While Malial and Dodd had targeted kids known to have family, Nneda and Cassie had slipped into the bowels of the province and taken delivery of the two sets of files.

She'd gotten so used to success that she missed the fact that it was all too easy. The documents had been made available just to bring her in.

"You've set me up," she said. The guard smiled. "The Realm never forgets."

Cassie felt cold then. She was going to die. Right now. Right here. They knew who she was, and they weren't going to take any chances. The guard was her judge, jury, and executioner.

With luck, this meant the real mission—saving the children—was unknown to the guards. If she played it well, a whole load of children might grow up to be the next fighters.

Around them, the G-12's control systems flashed in random flares of green and red. The presence of those children down in the cold transport section filled her up. She felt them, huddled in the cold, shaking, tears glistening, but clutching silence to their chests like it was a soft bear.

She felt Dodd, too, and Malial.

"Last words?"

She looked at Nneda.

"You know you can love more than one person, right?" she said.

The corner of Nneda's lip bent in a frown. A tear formed in the corner of her eye.

It was a standard between the four of them.

"I love you," one would say.

"You know you can love more than one person, right?" came the answer.

"Really?"

Then there'd be a smile, or a wink, or the simple raising of a suggestive eyebrow.

"Okay, then I love both you and me."

When shared between standard pair-mates accepted across the universe, it was a simple idea.

I love you before I love myself.

The fact that their bond included four commitments, however, and that their numbers, unlike the Artcurans, weren't needed for procreation itself, made them something different than the standard set of pair-mates. Add that their love wasn't constrained by gender or species, and it meant that by their mere existence they would be fighting the Realm forever. "You know you can love more than one *person, right?"*

That single sentence stood for the whole chain now.

Cassie pressed her lips together.

In the pregnant instant that followed, she clenched the seat rests and kicked the gun away. The guard held on to the weapon, but Nneda used the same moment to jump the guard that was watching her.

The momentum of both attacks caused the guards to crash into each other. They spun like tops in the zero-g of the cabin.

One of the weapons spun away and clattered against the G-12's control panel, whose lights were now flickering in mad, chaotic patterns that filled Cassie's brain with a rising crescendo of white noise.

Cassie grabbed the weapon as Nneda wrenched the other from the second tumbling officer. The movement sent new perturbations into the confusion.

One of the guards rose from his work with a comm-box, only to be accidentally kicked in the face by one of the other guards.

Then, suddenly, Dodd flew into the cabin with a wild body block into the fourth.

Cassie pushed off the wall, and shot the lead guard in a lower extremity, caroming into her, and sending the guard, screaming and gripping her leg, tumbling into the airlock. Nneda pistol-whipped her guard twice to create some space, then somehow flung the constable into the airlock, too— thudding at an awkward angle against the doorway, but falling in. Dodd had his guard pinned. The fourth was out like a light, floating motionlessly in mid-room.

A sudden blast from a vent in the cockpit pushed the unconscious guard toward the airlock. Nneda helped guide him there, and suddenly the lock door closed.

The final guard, seeing two guns trained on him, stopped fighting.

Dodd, panting with the exertion, kept him pinned by locking feet to the pilot's chair.

"What did you do that for?" Cassie said.

"What, save your life?"

Cassie glared at him, and Dodd hung his head in a way that let her know he understood. The Realm still had them locked down. In showing up, Dodd made it more likely they would search the whole ship.

"Maybe we shoot all four of them?" Nneda said.

Cassie's stomach dropped.

It made sense.

These guards had seen Dodd. The next set would certainly kill Cassie and Nneda, but they could still miss the children.

She looked at the fourth guard, whose eyes were slitted now.

Could she kill in cold blood?

Standing there, the G-12's com-channels pulsed in her head. Rather than raw noise, the lights on the control panels flashed in unison now. Her comm-link pulsed in a slow, strong, rhythm.

She swallowed. Her brows furrowed as the patterns of lights and pulses synched up, then flowed like a wave around the cockpit until the panels right before the pilot's seat flared.

The pattern repeated.

Then again.

"Tie him up," Cassie said, motioning the guard. "Then get the hell back to the kids and tell them to hold on."

She pushed her way to the pilot's seat and strapped in again.

Dodd did what he was told.

"What are you doing?" Nneda said, strapping in despite the question.

That's another thing she loved about these people. They understood that sometimes it was as important to act as well as to ask questions. She glanced at the guards in the airlock. She didn't know what they were going to do with them, but they would survive.

"I asked what's happening?" Nneda said.

"The ship's getting us out of here," Cassie said.

She didn't say more, but there was no doubt that the G-12 was talking to her now.

"Probably the AI," she said under her breath.

Yes. What would she do if she were stuck in the husk of a spaceship that sat in some nowhere boneyard? The AI had grown. The AI had learned from its records. Did it remember her? If so, did that mean the ship was alive?

She wasn't sure she wanted to go there, but now that she'd asked the question, Cassie felt something she was going to call conviction in the pulse of the ship now.

She felt familiarity.

Friendship. Or more than friendship. Trust. Compassion. Love?

"You know you can love more than one person, right?" she whispered under her breath as she readied the thrusters.

Really? The ship pulsed again.

"Yes," she replied.

Then, suddenly, every light around the control panel blazed at full brightness. A wave of warmth flashed from her shoulders down her back and throughout her entire body.

Then the panels went blank, and a comm-thread opened inside her mind.

It pulsed once, and the G-12's cannons leveled themselves at the Realm cruiser. It pulsed again, and two shots blasted out.

The restraints that had been holding their ship were gone.

"Hit it," Cassie said as the thread pulsed a third time.

Nneda did her thing.

The G-12 jumped.

Space Tyrants from the Void

Chapter 4: Cell Block Nebula, and The Fighting Tiger of Lakoo

appeared in *Boundary Shock Quarterly*
Ray Guns and Space Babes (Spring 2019) - #6

Okay, this one was just fun. When the "Ray Guns and Space Babes" guidelines essentially challenged us to go full pulp, I spent a whole day watching old SF serials just to get into the right mood. Then it was time to just let'er rip. I figured I was on the right path when Blaze labeled it as his "weirdest story." Or, at least I think it's the right path. You'll just have to decide for yourself on that one. But, yeah, it was great fun to write.

When we last saw Master Sergeant Jeff Cain, unbeknownst to his team of misfit mercenaries, he had suffered the full and horrific power of evil overlord Galaxian's GraviForce ray, a quantum beam that destroys the very fabric of the Strong Atomic Force that ties all matter together. The dissociated particle remnants of Cain's body were quark-locked in the nebulous entrails of Star-12 and its entire system, which had served as the target for Galaxian's test shot, spinning and careening wildly through the cold and vacuous void of space with so much energy that they yin-ed and yang-ed into and out of the multidimensions of a billion-billion universes, ever-expanding, radiating with gamma, alpha, and quantum vortices.

*Cain's mission had been to run a diversion so his crew
mates could sneak into Galaxian's fortress on the planet of
Lakoo, the secret base of Galaxian's Iron Empire. If they
don't corrupt Galaxian's computer systems, his forces will
use the GraviForce ray to take over the universe.*

*His only hope now, however, is his onetime sweetheart
Lieutenant Kij Wakefield—a brilliant Academy pilot who
was dishonorably dismissed from the Realm Defense
Command for hijinks that resulted in the destruction of
three hot-wired planet hoppers—and the rest of his team,
Heather and Dog-dog.*

*We join this story again as they race to board their latest
star jammer,* The Betty Bap.

On a dead run despite the oven-like heat of the planet,
Lieutenant Kij Wakefield threw herself into the pilot seat and
plugged directly into *Betty Bap*'s controls. Her sweat-
drenched shirt stuck to the chair, its smell already pungent
to her amped senses, her chest heaving with scorching
breath. The skin on her arms stood on full alert as her
nervous system linked up with ignition, power, and the
thruster computers.

The sweet, scouring release of data flowed through her
veins.

Betty Bap's external skin sensors were up.

Behind her, Heather clamored into the systems seat and
worked to get life support booted.

In the cliffs above, guards readied a tractor beam.

Mandibles clacking, and blaster hugged to his red chest,
Dog-dog raced down *Betty Bap*'s main passage toward the
secondary bay door, which was open on the opposite side of
the jammer hidden from the tower's sight. If things went
right, he would roll out of the bay door and hide while
Wakefield got the jammer flying away. Classic Cain plan—
draw attention to yourself while leaving the main attack
uncontested.

"Too close for comfort," Wakefield said, prepping the
boosters for final.

"All part of the plan," Heather snapped back, turning to

the task of getting *Betty Bap*'s systems up.

"Still too close."

Through the front screen, the top of the dark volcano at the edge of Galaxian's stronghold flared with a strong, brilliant strobe of neon blue that flashed up into space.

"I don't like the look of that," Heather said, blinking.

"Shut up and do your job," Wakefield said, agreeing with Heather's comment, but not wanting to hear it. An afterimage of the flare blurred her vision.

The whole goal had been to disable the weapon before it could be used. If Galaxian's ray gun had gotten off a shot, that could make for a very bad day.

Behind them, Dog-dog rolled out of the space craft.

As the bay doors clanged shut, Wakefield crammed the rocket driver forward. "Come on, little girl," she said to the jammer as the engines squalled and rocket fire bloomed as the *Betty Bap* rose off Lakoo's desolate floor.

"Hope Dog-dog leapt the right direction," Wakefield said, knowing that, if he hadn't, he was already roasted Dog-dog.

"If he toasted himself, I'll kill him," Heather screamed from the systems seat.

"Not if I kill him first," Wakefield replied, trimming up their roll.

The cockpit rattled and rolled.

The smell of rocket fuel overpowered any hint of charred man-cricket, though, so she gave up worrying and concentrated on getting this lovely piece of ancient history off the ground.

This was her element.

Cain was about making the right decisions, Heather was the brains, and Dog-dog found his way into and out of places like no one she'd ever seen. But flying a space jammer was Kij Wakefield's world—behind the yoke of a spaceship was the only place she felt comfortable.

As she guided the craft, thoughts raced ahead.

Dog-dog—they called him that because he was from the Sirius sector and because it pissed him off in a good way— was supposed to penetrate Galaxian's headquarters and install viral codes that would eat through the Iron Empire's communication tech to strip their automated weapons of their ability to coordinate.

When finished, he would take a twisty service path to the backside of the fortress, where Wakefield and Heather, having jumped back, would pick him up. Once that was done, they'd retrieve Cain from Star-12, and use the jammer's multi-d connection to Sag A* to do a black-hole jig back to Realm City, where they would pick up their paycheck and have a bit of a party.

That is: Wakefield, Heather, and Dog-dog would have a party.

Cain would probably go blow it all on kids from the Sisters of Holy Asteroid or some other such thing. Even now, Jeff Cain was a Master Sergeant at heart, and a hero at his soul—which meant he was a softie for Doing the Right Thing. He'd have taken this gig even if the Realm wasn't paying. Which was part of why she loved him so much—that and his smile, and ... well, a rise of interest made her push that line of thought aside. But, yes, he was gorgeous even before you accounted for the few mods he used, and he knew how to make people happy.

She'd loved Cain since the first time she saw him, and understood the opposite was true, too. When they were together, they were great. But she'd been open about her needs and about the way she saw love and people. She knew her desires. She understood the chemistry of her body.

If only he could accept her less than monogamous nature, he'd be perfect.

Alas.

He was who he was, and Heather's relentless suggestions for some of the more interesting genetics notwithstanding, Wakefield was sure that would never change.

It was Cain's rigid sense of loyalty that tied them together after all.

Each of them were Realm Defense washouts of a type: the Master Sergeant himself busted for refusing an wrongful order in an unjust system, Heather for blowing a whistle that shouldn't have been blown, Dog-dog for telling the wrong person he'd uncovered a conspiracy (how could he have known the colonel itself was involved?), and her, of course, for being too adventurous. They were all good at what they did, and Cain, with his still-hot connections with the brass and that healthy sense of righteous adventure that oozed out of his pores like a pheromone-laced aphrodisiac, made sure they always had more to do.

"Tell me again why we're doing this?" Heather quipped, watching the sensors register the movement of Galaxian's defense mechanisms.

"The benefits," Wakefield gave their pat response without adjusting her focus.

"Ah. Right. What are those again?"

"We get to save the universe."

Heather reached a foot to a pedal that adjusted the sight of *Betty Bap*'s laser, then fired a blast that took out the closest tractor beam station.

"Check," Heather said, arms flashing the fluorescent gold flare she'd installed from a fish on a tropical planet she'd visited as a kid.

As the *Betty Bap* rose through the air, a thud on the roof broke Wakefield's thoughts.

"Crap," she said, scanning the sensors and finding a muon tiger—a walking, semi-intelligent mound of atomic acid that ate organic material for breakfast 21 days a week—attached to the jammer's hull.

Galaxian's science guys had been doing double duty.

Wakefield pressed the thrusters, feeling the tiger's particle "claws" sinking, atom-by-atom, into the outer layers of the ship's protective shell. Another moment and the beast would rip the top off their jammer.

"Pulse field, Heather!" she called. "Now!"

"Whaddya think, I'm not working on it?" Heather said.

From the system seat, Heather crawled smooth hands over the control panel and dark-blue tentacles over other parts of its multi-colored pads.

"Not enough time," Heather said in a calm tone that betrayed the situation.

"Crap."

Wakefield had to shake the particle tiger before it took

down the whole plan—which meant she was going to have to get *Betty Bap* into the null-void now, which meant engaging the Galaxy Jump Drive before they got out of the planet's atmosphere.

In other words, shit was about to get hard.

"Strap in!" she yelled, pressing the drive stick forward.

The rotor churned up, and the hair on the back of her head rose.

The spaceship's structure warped and bent.

Composite metal surrounded them with a banshee wail.

Wakefield's stomach did loops as the craft's shuddering roar of blasting through airspace gave way to the smoothness of sliding through the null-void. White noise that sounded like sizzling bacon replaced the pounding of rockets.

Good girl, Wakefield said to herself.

As a jammer, *Betty Bap* was a small craft, so it made the jump quicker, which might have been all that saved them.

The null-void was a kind of interdimensional blank space that theoretically, at least, connected worlds from every dimension. Heather had tried to explain it to her one night over much alcohol, but she never fully understood the idea of extra dimensions as something more than a figment of a psychist's imagination. As far as she was concerned, until someone could actually fly to another world, they didn't exist. So the null-void was, to her, just a big kind of central station that let her jump a jammer from place A to place B without with all that messy Faster Than Light stuff that Heather thought was so interesting.

They couldn't stay there for long before the pressure warp would crush the ship, and, in fact, Wakefield could already feel the supports complaining. Usually they were just in and out, but now at least the null-void brought the muon tiger to a halt while Heather got to work.

Wakefield used a few seconds of the wait to put coordinates to Star-12 system into the astro-navigation system. Since they were here, might as well get Cain before going to grab Dog-dog.

By the time she was finished, the ship was nearly screaming in pain.

"Ready yet?"

"Almost."

She made an executive decision. "Keep working, but we gotta get out before we get squashed." Wakefield turned the stick to bring *Betty Bap* out of her Space-Time jump.

Full visuals snapped back as the ship came out of the null-void.

A look at the sensors told her that the muon tiger was still there—and was once again reviving itself, preparing to once again seep its "claws" through the hull.

"Crap," Wakefield said again. "Come on, Heather! Get that pulse field up now or we're going to be breathing vacuum."

Heather kicked the collider lever, and wrapped tentacles around the generator core beside the system seat, twisting it full strength.

The device hummed.

A pulse *whump*ed through the cockpit, rolled down the fuselage, then returned, ringing forward and aft with a whomping oscillation that sounded like an over-large tuning fork slowly dissipating. When the ship was finally quiet, Wakefield removed her hands from her ears and scanned the outer sensors to find the coast was clear.

The blast wouldn't kill the bastard, but it should have stung it good enough to keep it at bay long enough to get out of its segment.

"Good job," she said.

"It was in the bag the whole time," Heather replied, turning in the chair, their pink-irised eyes glittering and gleaming in that way that made it clear nothing had ever been really in the bag.

All four appendages relaxed, coiling across a well-cut 8-pack before Heather's hands wrapped clasped around them. The latest splice had provided motivation to work out and it showed.

Heather was both the brains of the group as well as its most liberal practitioner of genetic modification. It was hard to remember a time, however, when they took on any mod that didn't result in something visually pleasing—a fact that gave truth to the idea that even the smartest creature in the universe could be subject to a certain sense of vanity.

The tentacles had come from DNA procured on Garton-12. They were amazefab-and-doodle—as functional as they were sleek—almost amazefab-and-doodle enough to make Wakefield forget there was still work to do.

But not quite.

"We gotta get out of here before it comes back," she said, spinning to the pilot's controls and scanning the astro-navigation charts.

The Quantum Comm crackled then.

It was a scratchy voice blanketed in a steady blast of white noise.

Wakefield punched up the amplifier so the whole stream would be stronger, then applied a low band filter to get rid of static.

It was then she recognized the voice.

"Calling Lieutenant Wakefield," the voice was saying. "Calling Lieutenant Wakefield. Come in, Lieutenant Wakefield."

Over and over.

That the call came on QC channels didn't surprise her. Direct links through QC had the same "bypass the speed of light" advantages as it had for jammer jumping. But the fact that the voice was so weak made her freeze.

"Jeff?" she said. "Is that you?"

"It's me!"

"What are you doing?"

"I'm having a blast," the voice replied, stronger now, but only because the noise was being filtered.

"Where are you? Are you all right?" The image of the bright blue flash on Lakoo returned to her, and she shivered.

"If, by all right, you mean still mostly part of this dimension, I suppose so."

"Crap," Wakefield said.

"I think that's becoming your favorite word," Heather quipped.

"Shut up."

"Galaxian blasted me, Kij."

"Good god. How ...?" The words clotted in her throat. *How*

are you still talking? was what she had been about to say.

If Galaxian had hit Cain with the GraviForce ray, he should be deader than a neutron star.

"No time for that, Kij. I don't know what's happening, but I'm stuck in some kind of quantum state, half in this world, half in some other."

The idea made her head hurt.

"That makes sense," Heather said, standing up and coming forward to peer into the data screens.

"In what universe?"

The panel's lights fell over Heather's smooth skin. "The GraviForce ray has such intense power that when it rips matter apart, it could boost up the energy levels of those particles so far that they push out of our universe and into another." Heather looked at Wakefield, eyes wide. "I think the Master Sergeant is living in the quantum foam."

"Quantum foam?"

Heather shrugged. "Call it the null-void. It's the only environment where it would make sense that he's still in one piece."

"Crap."

Heather raised an eyebrow. Wakefield pursed her lips.

"The problem, though," Heather added, "is that once the energy levels of the particles fall, I'd guess he'll fall out of null-void and be done for."

"You mean he's going to cool down and die?"

"It would only make sense. His particles would fall out once he cools, and since in our space-time those particles are, um, scattered, that would probably be pretty bad."

"Crap. How much time?"

Heather shrugged. "Probably not much, but what do I know?"

"How do we find him? If we go into the null-void, can you get a spot on his location?"

"I doubt it."

Wakefield grabbed a helmet and stuffed the remnant of an EVA suit Cain had recently used into her belt loop, then stepped toward the air lock.

"What are you doing?" Heather said, tentacles coiling.

Wakefield pressed the helmet into place as she stepped into the lock, clipped into a thruster-pack, and grabbed a blaster.

Heather glared at her. "I asked a question."

Wakefield slammed the locking mechanism. The door irised shut, but not before she replied.

"Get the jump drive ready again. I'm going tiger hunting."

A moment later she was floating in space, one hand wrapped around the trigger mechanism of the blaster, the other twisting the controls of the thruster pack. Cain's EVA suit floated in zero-g. She took a position at *Betty Bap*'s tail just in time to see the muon tiger form up at the ship's mid-point.

"Here, kitty, kitty," she said.

The tiger stepped forward on six "legs," a mass of black and blue filled with silver static and bright flashes of sunlight-gold that made her think of colliders and positrons and quark patterns from some of her old physics books. She thought she could see individual muons pulsing across its outer layers. The beast sprouted heads and something she'd call teeth. The dead thuds of the thing's steps echoed through *Betty Baps*'s hull and through Wakefield's connection to the ship, dark and dull, making her feel like there was a weight to the thing.

She pulled Cain's suit from her loop.

The tiger paused.

The plan was to give the creature a bit of his DNA as a scent, and then follow it. Seeing the thing stalk her made her even more certain that chances that the plan worked were even slimmer than she had thought they might be.

"Screw it," she said, holding the suit toward the tiger. "I was never very good with math, anyway. Let's see if you've got a bit of bloodcat in you."

The beast launched.

Wakefield raised the suit between them, and sluiced the blaster around, sending a stream of plasma through the cloth and splitting the tiger at the same time. Particles of rayon and Kevlar mixed with free tiger muons and, as physics would have it, bits of Cain, too. Sweat and hair broke into individual molecules, dead skin cells left behind in crinkled elbow patches and knee braces dissociated into heat and ash, every molecule mattered.

The maw of the creature missed her, but its weight crashed into Wakefield, and she spun into free space.

The tiger recovered quickly, though.

An atomic burn seemed to grow deep in its solar plexus in blue and green pulses. It raised a black foreleg and prepared to attack.

Wakefield tried to hold her blaster steady as she used the thrusters to get back into control.

If this was the end, she was going to give as good as she took.

The beast hesitated as if thinking. As if puzzled. It twisted its head as if ... searching.

She wasted no time—pointing the thruster at the air lock and hitting full throttle. Her body crashed into the thick metal walls, and she hit the mechanism that closed the bay.

"Get the jump ready now," she said through the radio, not wanting to waste time. By the time she got to the pilot chair Heather had it heated up.

Outside, the tiger pulsed into the null-void.

Wakefield jammed the D-drive stick forward without even strapping in. *Betty Bap* screamed again, rolling and pitching as she jumped from a standing start into the sizzle of the null-void.

Wakefield grunted against the force.

She screamed, and finally plugged into the ship's systems.

"You're not getting away from me that easy!" she might have yelled at the beast.

She'd never followed anything in the null-void—never even knew it was possible. But she knew how to fly, and she'd been close with this little jammer long enough that she knew it inside and out.

"Come on, girl!"

Metal screeched as she banked the jammer left, then right to follow cadmium bold contrails of neon hues that had never been invented.

The beast was hungry and fast.

Wakefield had put it on the trail of prey.

How long would they run? How long could they last?

There, she thought, *ahead of the tiger,* as the beast ran true.

Cain was a perfect blue and purple void of human shape outlined in sparking lightning and the particle fire of the null-void. He crouched to meet the particle monster, his muscles bunching, his silhouette smooth and beautiful and suddenly so important to her that Wakefield thought she might cry.

For the first time since getting his message over QC, she let herself fall into the idea that she might one day live in a world without him.

And, as the tiger leapt at Cain, that idea destroyed her.

He wrapped one hand around the tiger's neck, the other around the beast's torso, holding it close to him, slick muscles bulging in flashing light.

The two tumbled like that, man and beast embroiled in a multidimensional death lock.

The void pulsed with energy.

The smells of a jungle tinged with a spice that might be ginger or cinnamon or burning sugar in the fields of Alebra III clutched at the back of her throat.

Betty Bap's hull gave a metallic cry and tossed to the left so hard Wakefield nearly lost her seat.

The ship was going to break up.

They were all going to die.

The image of Dog-dog waiting at the rendezvous flashed into her mind.

Then an explosion. Light. Crescendo of sound. The taste of fear.

Behind her, Cain's sweat-slick body fell to the floor.

Wakefield put everything into *Betty Bap*. Pulled the Gravity Drive stick hard. Up. Back.

Out.

Silence. Outside, nothing but a field of stars. Inside, now the ship pinged and groaned from strain.

Heather unbuckled. "Master Sergeant?"

Cain groaned and rolled to his side to vomit. When he was

done, he looked up from the floor.

"What are you waiting for? Let's go get Dog-dog."

Wakefield smiled, showing more relief than she was usually comfortable with.

"Get him strapped down," she said to Heather, then cranked the astro-navigator back to the coordinates of Lakoo's Iron Fortress.

She hit the rockets full thrust, and waited for *Betty Bap* to respond. As soon as both Cain and Heather were in seats, she pushed into the jump.

A hop later, they burst into Lakoo's atmosphere, coming in hard, but clean.

"Set us down there," Cain said, indicating a spot inside the fortress as he grabbed a blaster. "Now that we know the GraviForce ray works, we've got to go in and destroy the full mechanism," he explained.

She nodded, then set the jammer down in a cloud of dust.

"You're the best, Kij," Cain said as the dust cleared.

"Save it for later," Wakefield said, knowing he was right, but slid from the seat and steeled herself for their run into the fortress. They'd barely made it out last time.

Cain waved her back. "Heather and I will go."

"You're not leaving me," she said. "I'm not some lily—"

"We need you here," he said. "Dog-dog will be out soon, and we'll need to fly quicker than quick. We need you in the chair."

Wakefield cursed. "I hate it when you're right."

Cain smiled.

"Back in a minute," he said.

Heather wrapped tentacles around a set of four blasters, and followed.

The bay door gaped open and Cain bounded out, Heather right behind.

The silence they left behind was like a blanket. Like the air had left the cockpit.

Alone, Wakefield scanned the scene outside. Seeing no immediate sign of danger, she sat heavily in the pilot's seat and sighed, then ran a hand through her hair. It was tangled now. A matt of gold and brown she'd mixed from the natives on Plar.

She was tired, but happy. Suddenly able to breathe.

The remnant of Cain's physical presence was a thing here. She flashed on the image of him in the null-void. The sound of his voice over QC.

Could she love him enough to change?

Was it even possible?

Like Heather, and like Dog-dog, she'd tweaked so much of herself over the years—adding quickness and reaction time at the expense of nervous tics and developing bio-connects so she was better able to feel the spacecraft she loved to fly. Improved oxygen usage, more sensitive hearing, stronger muscle, self-moderated metabolism. Cosmetics, too, of course. Heather wasn't the only vain creature in their team. She loved her eyebrows and the slope of her jawline now. She'd change her hair again soon.

There was no gene for love, though.

At least not one she'd ever heard of.

But, if there were one, would she change herself to restrict who she could love? For Jeff Cain, would she become truly monogamous?

Or, turning the question, would she ask him to cut into his own DNA to become more accepting?

No, she thought.

Love is different.

It wasn't Cain's fault that he didn't understand her attractions, just as it wasn't her fault that she had them. In the end, they were like a pair of binary stars, bound together in orbits that they couldn't break, but that also meant they could never really connect. The image made her feel good in the way that the last rays of a sunset did.

Love was like gravity, not DNA.

If she and Cain were ever going to happen, she wanted it to be real.

The sound of approaching footsteps broke her daydreaming.

Wakefield turned to see Dog-dog fall through the primary bay door and land on the floor with a dead thud.

"You were expecting him, right, Lieutenant Wakefield?"

She stared into the eyes of the overlord of the Iron Empire, who stepped into the *Betty Bap*'s hold, orange cape swirling.

"Galaxian," she said as several guards filed into *Betty Bap*, blasters trained directly on her.

"At your service." He smiled. "Or shall I say, you're under arrest?"

She punched. She clawed. She bloodied several, and even grabbed a blaster from another, and was just raising to take aim when one guard pressed a hypo to her neck.

As her vision grew dark, Wakefield felt the pull of gravity.

That brings us to the end of this exciting segment of Space Tyrants from the Void*! Will Lieutenant Kij Wakefield survive? Is Cain still alive? If so, can he save her from Overlord Galaxin's evil clutches, and can they ever find true love that lasts?*

Join us at this same theatre next week when we present Chapter 5: Mountain Disaster and the Space Chains of Doom*!*

Eyes Flashing Blue and Brown and Green

appeared in *Boundary Shock Quarterly*
Apocalypse Descending (Summer 2019) - #7

I wrote a very early draft of this one several years back, after having visited Kentucky's Mammoth Cave with my family. It's a beautiful place—these long, infinitely winding caverns that have carried water and air through the surrounding areas for as long as they've existed. Native Americans used them. Armies in the Civil War used them. Spelunkers explore them today. The caves, if you let your mind wander, can extract all sorts of different emotions.

Anyway, like I said, I wrote the bones of this one way back then, and even then, though it was spare, I liked the whole point behind it. Then the Apocalyptic theme came around and my mind...er...flashed on this one. I fished it out of the mire of my memory, and figured out why it wasn't working. Well, I figured it out for myself, anyway. Feel free to tell me I'm outta my mind wrong. Given its birthplace, I find myself smiling when I think of it. Hopefully it will speak to you, too.

It turns out that all it takes for humans from around the globe to *want* to work together is an annihilating force from the stars appearing on the Terran doorstep.

PFC Pravin Rodrigo Kulkarni, a man born of a Spanish mother and East Indian father, reconned the woodsy hillside with his platoon mates—Jack Hung to his left, Illira Hendrickson slipping along the brambles on his right, the rest spread out along the line. Their company had been together for nine months, and in the field for most of that.

In most ways, Pravin was already closer to these people than he was to his family, something that surprised him every time he thought about it.

Their mission today was simple: climb the hill, confirm reports of an Antarean ground landing, and provide reconnaissance to feed their intel folks.

Progress was simple enough: Deliberate steps, one foot in front of the other, watch your mates, keep your gaze on the brush that grew out of the forest.

It was a tense slog, though.

A hard rain earlier this morning had cleaned the air of its bombed-out smell, leaving only the oaks' and sycamores' earthy aromas under the dark canopy of green, which Pravin liked. The dampness of the aroma made it like being back home, but it also left the ground wet and hard to walk over while maintaining silence—especially with thick-legged elephants in the company like Parks, who Pravin could hear from three slots over. They worked together, though, picking their way through tangled trunks.

Sharp sweat ran salty on Pravin's lips. A trail of the same ran down his temple to tickle alongside his ear.

It was a strange place, America.

A place that, a mere two weeks before his twenty-third birthday, he'd have never thought of being in. But, then, everything was strange now.

The 115th International was assigned out of Fort Knox and responsible for the defense of what had once been Western Kentucky. He found the woods here to be different from back home in that, hard rain aside, the land was dry most of the time. Mangalore, where Pravin was from, was true rain forest. He understood what real rain was.

The humidity here reminded him of home, though.

Summer in Kentucky was also like breathing through a sponge.

Suddenly, something bothered him.

He halted and raised his hand, and his team mates right and left froze in place.

For the hundredth time since leaving camp this morning, Pravin missed his TP—the small computer system each soldier carried inside their skulls. The TP had brought them all together in ways no one had thought possible, literally connected every brain in the company to keep them in constant contact. It was still inside his head, of course, but like everyone else's it had gone TFU—Totally Fucked Up—on the first of the Antareans' pulses. The upper brass said that the code heads and chip guys were working to see if they could reboot them, but none of the boots on the ground thought it had a chance in hell of working again, and nothing but a crow bar or a surgeon's knife would be able to dig it out now.

Pravin hoped that wouldn't be happening any time soon.

From across the wood, Jack Hung's expression carried the question. "What is it?"

Pravin narrowed his eyes and raised his rifle—on old-style projectile automatic rather than the plasma throwers that had also gone TFU. He silenced his breathing, trying to determine what it was that had gotten him spooked. The weight of his pack pressed on his shoulders heavy as sin.

The woods here were always quiet in the way a good forest was quiet, meaning that a steady hum of bird call, leaf rustle, and scurrying creatures filled his ears.

But no birds chattered now.

No animals chuffed in the distance.

It was late enough in the afternoon, too, he should probably be hearing the first screeching of frogs from the creeks and ponds that fed the complicated morass of caves that ran below the surface here. Mammoth Caves, the Americans called them. Which made sense, even given the Americans' propensity to name everything in gargantuan terms. Just the idea of uncounted miles of cave beneath their feet made Pravin's mind twist. The idea of them gave him a sense of permanence, a feeling that humanity could win this thing, that sometime the Antareans would grow tired of the bombing or just mine out whatever they wanted, and that then they would leave.

These caves had been here forever, after all.

He hoped, when this was all over, that he would be able to explore them.

Right now, though, he worried.

"It is too silent," he finally whispered, hyper-aware of how he pronounced every word.

Hendrickson drew her eyebrows together in the way Pravin knew she did when she was accessing the TP. It made him miss the touch of her thoughts. Coming up empty, she frowned and tried to listen.

"I think you worry too much," she whispered back.

Pravin stifled a chuff.

When you grow up in a place where your home is an open shack with two walls of cardboard and two more of scrap tin, you learn how to both listen and worry. Pravin had once won a bucket of beer by spending most of a sentry detail with his eyes closed and tracking an individual woodpecker from the sound of its beak pounding against trees. "How do you do that?" one of his mates had said as he paid up. Pravin grinned. For him, the woodpeckers were odd little birds. The staccato echoes they made were like distant movements in the slums he'd lived in before his brother got the job that let him buy the family a small house in the city.

Now, though, the forest was as hushed as a symphony house, and he couldn't tell why.

He turned to wave Hung and Hendrickson to back off.

The bomb came before he could finish.

It was an orange flash.

An ear-ringing blast of sound.

It was stone and wood and soil that rose like a wall of saw-teeth.

Jack Hung was ahead of him one moment, gone the next.

A force lifted Pravin up like it was connected directly to his gut. He tumbled away, flying, arms whirling, then hitting the ground, screaming, bouncing, and tumbling until he crashed hard into a tree stump.

For an instant everything was so still and so silent that Pravin thought maybe he was dead. Maybe he was looking at a painting. The pressure on his ears and throat made him feel like he was under water. *Pretty*, he thought as he looked at the green and orange scene before him.

He wanted to say something but his brain couldn't come up with it.

Finally, he took a breath.

The pain hit a moment later—a acidic sharpness that burned from his ribs and a hammer blow heat from his left leg, which was bent at an odd angle, and from which blood had already began to soak crimson stains through his fatigues.

Shit.

He tried to lift his head, but pain was a firebrand burning from inside.

Shit, shit, shit.

"Parks!" he yelled, realizing his own voice barely registered in his blown-out hearing. There was no answer.

"Jack!" Still nothing.

He ran off a string of names: Yi, Javarian, Assan, Jackson.

No one answered.

He glanced left and right.

The smell of burnt carbon was everywhere, and the sight of flames crackling as they ate at living trees helped him triangulate his hearing, which seemed to be coming back as sure as his pain had.

Sucking another breath, he turned his gaze to the open hole in the canopy of the woods around them. The Antareans were nothing if not systematic. One of their airships would come next. If it found him like this, he was dead.

A boulder sat a short distance away.

Cover. He had to hide.

He turned himself over, crying against the pain as he crawled on his belly until he was behind the rock. He lay back, working hard just to breathe the thick air.

In the sky above the green line of trees, one of the horseshoe-shaped monstrosities the Antareans used as advanced killing machines glided into his vision.

The lander would not be far behind.

Under normal circumstance his TP would have pinged when the drone first came into range, a thought that made him mad. This was his fault. He'd felt the problem before it came. If they'd had a head's up, his company could have taken cover. He should have known. Should have reacted earlier.

But then, couldn't they all have said that?

Some will argue that the change in humanity began shortly after the Antareans appeared on astronomers' scans, but that would be wrong. It almost got serious after diplomats opened communication channels, and before the visitors made it to the solar system, but that, too, is giving us a little too much credit.

True cooperation between humans happened only when the Antareans ignored those queries, and merely pressed onward toward our home. Only after the space boys couldn't keep the bugs outside Saturn's orbit did it register to the average joe on the street that the Antareans weren't here to build trade routes and beam us up.

Suddenly, no one cared if you were from England, or Beijing, or the States, or even Pravin's own Mangalore, India.

Generators and medical supplies appeared as if by magic.

Autos, planes, and construction equipment were suddenly everywhere.

As were intelligence and know-how.

Builders taught other builders. Politicians agreed with other politicians.

Still, the Antareans pressed on, confirming their intent by silently entering Earth orbit. The world had discovered exactly how much it had to give to each other, but now had so little time.

Terra's collective scientists—who called themselves Geek Platoon—targeted the entire network of satellites in near Earth orbits at the Antarean mother ship, but all they managed to do was flame a few escorts.

The first wave was a swarm of landers.

The IAF was able to stop a few as they entered the atmosphere, but the Antarean numbers were large and each mission lost planes at an obscene ratio.

The second wave came shortly after.

Pravin and his mates ran a battery of laser-powered particle guns they dubbed Triple B for "Betty the Bug Blaster."

The battle was the most gut-wrenching twenty minutes of Pravin's life.

Fire filled the bright blue sky. Antarean craft flew with the sound of fried eggs, and burned with grey smoke. When the battery scored a kill, the ground thundered when the slag of those ships crashed to the Earth in great balls of flame. What few planes the Terrans still had screamed in low-altitude combat.

When the sky had finally gone clear, they had survived.

Pravin and his mates gave each other rousing cheers and great slaps on the back.

Take that, motherfuckers, they had said.

The Earth was ours.

There was celebration. Drinking and hugging and more drinking.

He had never felt more alive.

Pravin still had a picture of that day stored on his TP.

They were designed to record everything that happened, after all, and that day most definitely happened. After each mission, each soldier was supposed to link and download everything for a rapid sharing and intel analysis. When the download was finished, each soldier was supposed to wipe their base memory so they could store more. He had kept this image rather than dump it, though, because it made him feel good and because he figured sec-ops wouldn't kick him too hard for holding onto a few bits of data.

The image was clear and vivid.

It showed the young men of his platoon—Hendrickson, Ali, Jason, Yi—their eyes flashing blue and brown and green, their skins knitted together like camouflage colored with the flush of success. He remembered that moment, feeling the depth of their thoughts and the warmth of their arms across his shoulders.

The first EMP attack hit less than an hour after that photo was captured, disabling pretty much everything electronic.

Then came the real bombing.

Pravin lifted his right leg. It was almost good.

He could probably hobble a bit if he needed to, but he didn't want to need to.

From his perch behind the boulder, Pravin watched the landers arrive, each dropping multiple tethers that each supported a hundred or more bugs. He scanned the ground around him, hoping to find a way to report this status. The platoon lay dead around him. If he stayed here, the Antareans would find him.

A slit of darkness split the ground a few feet away.

A cave opening, maybe—three feet wide and a foot high.

His training kicked in and he thought of the network of caves below.

Maybe he could slip into one and find his way back to base. If he had his TP, he was almost certain he could, but that wasn't the case. He peered at the dark hole. It sat there silently, taunting him. He thought of his hometown when he was a child. A tiny patch of darkness in the nighttime. A twisted morass of haphazard paths and alleyways. Dirt floors.

The landers were coming closer now.

Bugs had no resistance of any merit.

He edged closer to the opening and dropped a handful of dirt into the gap. It fell only a few feet, safe enough. He dropped his rifle in, then gasped in pain as he gripped the rock at the entrance lip, slid into the hole, and dangled for a moment before dropping to the floor.

Blistering sheets of white filled his vision on impact of landing.

When the pain receded, he found himself in a small chamber with smooth limestone walls. Water trickled somewhere in the distance, and a sweet breeze of fresh air came from the darkness within.

Another barrage of bombs rattled the ground above.

Grit and dust filtered down from the slit in the ceiling, reminding Pravin that he was committed now. Pain or no pain, he wasn't going to be able to climb out of this place.

He used his rifle to get to his feet.

The floor was dry.

Fighting the urge to scream out with each movement, he flipped the light switch on his helmet on, leaned hard on the butt of his rifle, and limped in the direction of fresh air.

The cool temperature made him recall a conversation in which he and a guy from Alabama worked to convert Imperial to metric.

His torchlight splayed across stone walls.

A rodent scampered off. As he progressed, an occasional cave cricket or white millipede, oddly hunched and colorless, scurried away, their antennae wriggling in the darkness, eyes big and wide to take in every photon that happened to arrive.

At one time he used to think bugs and creatures were the same everywhere, but he soon discovered his experience was limited to spiders and cockroaches, dogs and donkeys, and those few monkeys who smoked cigarettes and played hide-and-seek with fresh mangos in Rakesh's corner show.

Until a year ago, he would have considered these cave creatures to be alien life-forms in themselves.

The caves themselves were like another world to him. The veins of minerals and crystals could have come from exotic planets in other worlds.

Sunil, his eldest brother, would have loved it here.

Sunil was the one who had wanted to excavate relics, after all, or study volcanic plains, or any one of a hundred other dreams that are common among young men interested in exploration and adventure. As he edged forward, Pravin thought of the word *spelunker,* which he had never known existed before coming here.

As he grew up, Pravin himself had been content to merely paint the sunset over their home in Mangalore. But if Sunil were still alive when this came to its end, Pravin decided that he would bring him here. He would point to this cave and say to his brother, "See, Sunil. I told you I was a spelunker when I was in the services."

His rifle tip slipped in a crack and he only managed to remain standing because he fell against a slab of limestone.

Collecting his breath, Pravin cursed himself for letting his mind wander.

A misstep in the darkness could be fatal.

He tried to concentrate on the cave, but his head swam.

He was losing blood, he thought as he purposely avoided looking at his mangled leg. Each step brought fresh bursts of pain, and he fought the need to hyperventilate. He tried to access his GPS, but his TP was no better now than it had been moments and weeks ago.

He swallowed, trying to feel which way the air current was moving. His chances of surviving were fading.

Pravin stopped to admonish himself for the thought.

His parents had not raised a quitter.

Other people had suffered worse and lived.

He clenched his hand over the butt of his rifle and braced himself as he took another careful step. He came to a place where the passage fell away. The light on his helmet seemed to be dimmer, too, though he couldn't be sure if it was that or if his vision was fading. He shivered, too, his muscles growing hard against the chill.

He limped on.

The tip of his rifle slipped in a liquid pool, and Pravin lost his balance.

He fell hard and slid down a wet incline, pain cutting like freezing acid until suddenly he was in freefall. His ribcage hit rock and fresh pain fired across every nerve in his body.

He clenched his eyes shut for a long time, trying to control his breathing.

As he calmed, the faint trickle of water came to him.

The air smelled clean.

When finally he could open his eyes, he found himself wedged into a small crevasse at the bottom of a short shaft. His pelvis was stuck, his hands free, and the rifle that had been his walking cane was wedged on a rock formation several feet above him. Light from his helmet fell on smooth rock formations that were milky white and laced with brilliant orange—stalactites flowed from the ceiling and stalagmites rose like giant pikes.

Water glistened from its surface.

The chilly atmosphere of the cave cooled his body.

Pravin tried to move, but could not.

He shouted, but there was no one to hear.

He was bleeding to death.

Pravin Rodrigo Thakkar, a man born of a Spanish mother and an East Indian father, was bleeding to death in a cave that he had just learned had been discovered by Native Americans thousands of years earlier, but had been formed by the power of the universe over millions of years. He bled into cloth made in San Francisco. Equipment made in Malaysia was affixed to his temple. His helmet, crafted in Dusseldorf, would provide him light for several more hours.

A gun manufactured in China lay on a rocky shelf two meters away.

He was done.

He had not been as strong in his faith as his mother had wanted him to be, but now, as his feet tingled in the cold and as the stone was hard against his fingers, Pravin wondered what would happen next.

He thought about hours. He thought about months and years and decades and millennia.

One of the other things he'd learned about caves is that decomposition occurs slowly here. Cave insects, pack rats, bats, and a hundred other creatures gnaw at rotting flesh slowly.

The water here carries a solution of calcium and carbonic acid from the limestone above. The air draws carbon dioxide from that mixture, and as the water evaporates it leaves behind bits of calcium to latch onto bone. He wondered if it would form over his helmet and the prefab uniform he wore, too. If left long enough, perhaps it would build another one of these strangely alien formations that lay around him.

He thought of himself as a monument encased in stone.

His stomach churned.

The TP blipped then.

A single *fitz*, a lone fire of static that made him jump so hard he cracked his helmet against the rock behind him. His heart beat like a locomotive. He tried to access the unit again, and again got a fizzling stream of white noise.

The image stored on its memory flashed in his mind then: young soldiers, his friends, their eyes flashing blue and brown and green.

It was nothing, really. Nothing useful.

Yet it was everything.

He was here. His people were here.

The thought that the blip was a random fact of electrical devices crossed his mind, but he dropped it first thing. Geek Platoon had succeeded. He had to believe that, had to believe that the combined power of all of humanity had found a way. Because that's what matters, he thought. If Geek Platoon had been successful, they'd come for him. And when they retrieved him, he was going to remember this moment. People live to find a way: for themselves, for their families, and for each other.

He took a breath, braced against the rock, then pushed upward, putting every ounce of energy he had into dredging himself out of the crevasse. His flesh gouged against sharp rock. Blood ran. His scream echoed in the cold caverns. He gained not much. An inch, maybe.

Gasping, he pushed again.

His arms shook and his muscles felt like they would tear, but his legs came free, and he flopped out onto the surface of the ridge, where he lay panting with his cheek against the cold rock for some time. He tasted dirt and dust. Felt the cold of the world underneath him suck heat from his body.

From the corner of his eye he saw a hunchbacked cave cricket scamper away.

Finally ready, Pravin reached for his rifle and dragged himself to his feet. After leaning against the rocky surface for a moment, he was ready to face the caves again.

As he took a step, the TP flared.

Goliath's Sling

appeared in *Boundary Shock Quarterly*
Asteroid Miners and Comet Wildcatters (Fall 2019) - #8

The prompt this time had us deal with the realities of working in space as we know it and love it today. None of the highfaluting faster-than-light stuff, right? Just hop into a tin can and get thee hence to Mars or Venus or the asteroid belt or, well, you get the drill. Against this backdrop I recalled one of my early memories: listening to my dad read Jack London's "To Build a Fire," which is a classic story of man vs. nature.

When we get to a point where human beings are living in space—and I do mean truly living in space, working and loving and playing and fundamentally living out a life in the darkest regions of Deep Space—I think the earliest days (centuries?) are going to be like that: amazing, heart-wrenching, uplifting, and devastating all at the same time. You're on your own out there. To the victors will go the spoils, of course. But when something goes wrong it will be just you and the horses that brought you, and the line between life and death will sometimes be impossible to define.

"I'm activating my environmental suit," Paul Daniels said more for the data recorder's benefit than anything else.

"Marking it now," Roger Martin replied from ZC—Zone Control.

An icy rock loomed ahead of Paul's pusher, spinning through space like a giant snowball. At something over two hundred thousand tons of ice and ore, this one would probably pay for the rest of Heather's education.

His spacecraft was essentially a single-seater, small in comparison to the ice ball, like David to Goliath, not much more than an empty can bolted onto a fuel tank the size of a full-length spaceport shuttle. They had three of the things back at ZC, specifically designed for Oort cloud mining. The pushers were old equipment, and about the only thing on board that could be guaranteed to work right were the data recorders that monitored every movement a pilot made.

Wouldn't want a miner to win a lawsuit, you know.

Paul shrugged and shook out his hands. It was a nervous habit he'd affected back when he was a kid. It helped center himself and get rid of stress.

The pusher had drifted a degree and a half, so Paul toggled lateral thrusters to correct the approach. The claws came into alignment with the steel connector he had fired into the rock earlier, a mechanism that consisted of a flat plate with a raised, circular ridge placed directly in the center of the ice ball's axis of rotation. Paul guided the claws closer, syncing the latching claws with the magnetic signature of the connector's wobble to allow the machine to correct for any misplacement of the connector. This was the critical moment—an error here could knock the rock into a different spin, thereby requiring a new latching base and a standard week of work.

It was a week Paul couldn't afford if, like he had promised, he was to have any chance of making it home for Heather's birthday.

Once the claws fully attached, he would stabilize the whole system and turn the pusher to point the rock in the right direction. Then he would light the primaries, and send the thing sunward with a massive thruster boost. After a several year journey, a processing station would grab the rock and break it into its constituent parts for use as rocket fuel and for support of various Martian and Lunar cities.

It was meticulous work, and dangerous if you weren't

careful. Physics were a heartless bitch when you were
essentially alone out in deep space. The government said
every mining station was supposed to be occupied by a
minimum of three people. But Chi Huang ditched out last
month, and the company hadn't yet managed to find a
replacement. So now it was just Roger in ZC and him out in
the piece of shit crate his company flew.

There was supposed to be money for new equipment next
year, but Paul wasn't holding his breath, and until they did
get new stuff these antiques reminded him of the junkers
he'd tried to move back when he helped his dad sell second-
hand spacecraft on the junk lot.

All said, he didn't really mind, though.

Pilots made a lot more than button pushers did.

Besides, he enjoyed the constant tinkering, figuring out
what problem needed fixing, and how to make repairs. It was
something he was good at.

He tapped the thruster pad, coaxing the pusher closer. His
screen flashed a green icon. The claws had acquired the
connector's spin pattern and the computer had calculated
the appropriate latching parameters. "I've got a go for latch,"
he said into his radio.

"Sounds good, Paul," Ray replied from ZC. "Grab the
mother and let's get a move on."

Paul opened the claws, and his pusher edged forward.

A loud bang echoed through the pusher, and the entire
unit lurched sideways. A thruster had just let loose. He
punched the reverse retros, but it was too late and the
competing forces of his engines unleased all hell. The claws
engaged, crashing into the connector plate and the raw
surface of the ice ball to freeze in place and act as a lever.

His thruster correction worked against him.

Electrical wiring ripped.

The pusher cockpit thrashed, throwing Paul against
restraints so hard that he thought they'd cut through his
shoulder.

The arm had not been designed for lateral stress, and it
buckled under the combined masses of the pusher and the
snowball.

The pod whipped left, then right.

Metal tore.

The pusher crashed back into the rock with a crystalline shower of ice spray and debris of what he hoped wasn't his spacecraft.

Then it was over.

The rock drifted on its way, the torn remnant of the latching arm and connector jutting from its surface like a mangled golf flag. And the pusher, crumpled and powerless, shot through space like a bullet from Goliath's sling.

The vacuum buzzer rang inside Paul's helmet, meaning the external hull had been breached. Buttons across the panel screamed in pulsing red flashes.

"Ah, shit," he said.

His shoulder throbbed where the straps of his restraining harness had held him in.

He turned off the siren.

The thrusters didn't respond to his prompts, so he toggled the retros and checked the power system.

Still nothing but red lights.

"Jesus, Paul, are you okay?" Roger's voice came through his ear pod.

"Not sure yet," Paul replied as he unclipped himself from the pilot's seat and twisted his arm to work out some of its soreness. "Main power's out and I've got no engines. External vacuum is breached, and my suit mechs have completed the seal. Bottom line, I got a damned good whacking."

"All right, I'm coming to get you."

"Thanks," Paul replied.

He slipped out of the chair and checked out the tiny rear compartment.

"Almighty mother of God," he said under his breath.

The entire ass end of the ship was gone, and where the fuel cell used to be was now just an open hole ringed with torn metal and long white straps that floated in space like thick strands of plastic spaghetti. Those straps had just moments ago held a small emergency supply of oxygen, enough for maybe an hour. But now the emergency tanks, as well as the huge fuel cell, were spinning somewhere out in space.

He glanced at his own oxygen level.

Plenty of time left, assuming Roger could come get him.

"The entire aft end is gone, Roger. The oxygen system and fueling equipment are separated."

"Can we dock?"

"Let me look." Paul grabbed a handrail and pulled himself cautiously to the other side of the derelict craft. "Yeah, I think so. The ring appears to be fine."

"Good. Sit tight."

Paul could almost see his partner sliding into the second pusher.

"Sitting tight," he replied. What the hell else was he supposed to do?

"Shit," he said to himself. Beth would have his short hairs if he didn't manage to make Heather's birthday, and now there was a very real possibility he was going to miss it.

The trip Earthside from the Oort cloud was a standard month at best, and it would take at least five days to make up for their lost time.

He bit his lip.

Beth had loved the idea of dating a pilot back when they had met, but things had changed, and no talking could make her see that the money he made on this job would be enough for him to retire in his mid-fifties if they managed things right. There would be plenty of time to be together after that.

If she could just hold on another ten years.

He grimaced, feeling the lie beneath his rationalization.

Paul had struggled with this his entire life. First it was the decrepit junkyard that had kept his dad Moon-locked all his life and that his dad had wanted him to take over.

That would have worked fine for Beth, too, of course. Once they were married, Beth had wanted him to stay at home. Not a completely unreasonable request, but Paul couldn't do that. He was a pilot. He'd always been a pilot. It's what made him who he was.

They had talked about this before the wedding, but apparently it hadn't really set in.

Beth said she could handle it, but in truth she never seemed to understand what keeping him home would mean. Not that he really blamed her. It was hard for him to describe it himself.

Since Heather had been born, though, Beth had shown outright anger toward his job, exposed her fear that Heather would grow up without a father.

Paul, himself, had always pushed that fear aside.

A man doesn't survive space if he lets thoughts like that get under his skin.

"I'm at fifteen hundred meters and closing," Roger's voice echoed in Paul's ear. "Looks like you've been given a pretty good ride, my friend. But I think we can dock all right."

Paul watched as the second pusher moved in tighter.

He and Roger had been friends since the Academy, Roger being the only cadet who could out fly him one-to-one. Both had spent more than one occasion in the director's lounge being informed that joyriding in the Academy's space craft could do long-term damage to one's career.

As if they had cared.

They had been twenty-one years old and could barely conceive of making a mistake, better yet being less than invincible.

Now, though, they both had a little less hair and a few more wrinkles. And they had seen enough of space that they even followed most of the company's safety procedures. Roger had been his best man, and Heather had always called him "Uncle." For his part, Roger ran a steady string of women past him and Beth, all being declared by Beth as being "unworthy" of him.

The two of them had agreed to mine this chunk of space because it looked like a surefire winner. And it had been. But there was more to it than profit, and Paul knew it. The idea of being on the edge of the solar system looking in made him feel something special. And the dark shadows in Beth's gaze let him know that she fully understood it was something she could never give him. That Roger had the same flare made it worse, and probably also served as the reason they could never keep a third member around long enough to get comfortable.

Chi, for example, had never seen the role as anything but a job.

The impact of Roger's docking maneuver broke Paul from his thoughts.

A dull thud traveled through the ripped-up structure and into his suit.

"Knock, knock," Roger said.

"Who's there?"

"Commode."

"Commode who?"

"Commoder here and hold the other end of this docking station, asshole."

Paul groaned. "Jesus, Rog. Maybe I'll get you a decent sense of humor for your next birthday."

"That's what you said last year."

"Actually, I could use a hand with the data recorder."

Paul moved back to the cockpit. The unit would help prove that the thruster had gone bad, and that he hadn't destroyed the equipment through any slight of his own hand.

Nice, for once, to be able to turn the tables.

"On my way."

Roger's movement echoed faintly through his pusher's structure. His hand gripped the edge of the entryway, and he half-stepped and half-pulled himself through the docking tube.

The docking mechanism was designed with a system of magnetic clamps that latched and held the boot ring of the connection tube—sensors detected a good seal, then relayed messages back to the pusher's central controller.

Undocking was a similar function, the sensors indicating when the latch had been disconnected, and sending messages to the controller to let it know the tube should be withdrawn.

The accident, however, had done damage that neither Roger or Paul had been able to see.

Metal around the boot ring crumbled when the third latch connected. Still, there had been enough pressure there to register a successful connection.

And Ray had moved into the tube.

As he struggled in zero-g, his boot struck the inner wall of the tube, which jolted the passageway enough that the faulty latch lost hold. The sensor sent a message to the controller. And the controller responded.

One side of the tube tried to withdraw.

The other side remained latched.

A loud crack, sharp and clean as an ice break, came through Paul's suit.

The docking rim on Paul's pusher buckled inward, and the accordion-like tunnel crumpled under sudden strain. A metallic tearing ripped through the ship.

Roger screamed over the radio, his voice ragged with fear as the two spacecraft came together, crushing Roger between them.

He never had a chance.

"Oh, shit," Paul said over and over again, panicking for the first time. "Oh, shit, oh shit, oh shit..."

The ships drifted apart.

Roger's mangled body floated in still silence, half inside Paul's pusher and half in the void. A rolling light crawled over his yellow suit like a horizontal line over a dead video screen.

It took Paul a moment to realize the strobe was light from the open airlock door on Roger's pusher as it spun away from his craft.

Paul grabbed his friend's body and pulled him inside.

He searched Roger's cracked faceplate, hoping to see some sign of life. But his expression was so pale and rubbery Paul knew he was dead even before checking the suit's monitor for vital signs.

Outside the open airlock door, the healthy pusher drifted away.

He had to get himself onto that spacecraft soon, or he was going to end up just as dead as Roger.

He glanced at his oxygen meter, something under forty minutes.

Paul didn't know what to do with his friend. Theoretically, he could leave him floating free in the compartment, but that just didn't feel right. His eyes set upon the pilot's seat. Without further thought, he pushed Roger into it and ran straps around him.

Outside, the second craft continued to rotate, revolving maybe once every five seconds, slowly drifting, now some fifteen meters away. His own pusher was rotating counter to Roger's.

The cadence of his breathing rose and fell.

Without power in his own ship, Paul realized he had only one possibility.

He would have to jump.

He would have to leap into the void, timing things just right to coincide with the second pusher's rotation so that he would be able to get into the airlock entrance.

Fear traced an arc down his spine.

If he missed, Sir Isaac Newton said he would just keep going, falling into deepest space until his air ran out, slowly suffocating. A cold pit grew in his stomach. He would eventually stop, of course, slowing in the weak gravity well of the sun to become another piece of space debris in the Oort cloud.

"Stop it!" he said to himself. "Just stop it."

His arms hung loosely at his side and he shook them to deal with anxiety that was suddenly permeating everything he did.

He set his jaw, giving his body a moment to affect a professional calmness.

Even if he made it into the second pusher and got the ship turned back to ZC, he had a problem. The airlock tube in that second pusher was destroyed, and without its presence, the doors wouldn't open unless someone inside the station gave the command. And, of course, there was no third.

One problem at a time, he thought. Standard Academy training. Deal with one problem at a time.

He watched above him, waiting for the second pusher to rotate slowly into view, which it did a second later.

Its airlock seemed tiny in the distance.

Paul watched as the first "launch window" passed, using this cycle, and then another, to judge timing.

By now the pushers were easily twenty meters apart.

Sweat beaded on Paul's brow, and he tried not to look into the bottomless blackness that surrounded him. His pusher rotated with excruciating slowness as the healthy pusher's opening appeared, twisting slowly to disappear from the bottom side of the craft, then reappear on the topside. He coiled his legs and sprang.

It was spinning too fast, he thought as he flew through space.

The opening would pass him by.

He was going to miss.

He stretched as he flew toward the pusher, miraculously grasping one edge of the airlock with the fingers of one open hand and holding on with everything he could muster. His muscles strained, and his fingers felt like they would rip as they held the lip of the bat. His body mass whipped around the pivot, and Paul crashed against the rounded surface of the pusher so hard he lost his breath.

Just as miraculously, he did not let go.

Gulping air, Paul reached up with his other hand to balance himself, then, once he was stable, he performed a reverse somersault into the open airlock cavity. Quickly, he activated the controls.

The door locked in place and the cabin pressurized.

He immediately went to the high-gain radio.

"All points emergency. This is Paul Daniels, mining in Zeta sector. I have an emergency situation with one death confirmed. I need help. Please hail." That would do it for now, he thought. His plea would take an hour to get to the guys at the Katani Control Station, and he could add more information when he got back to ZC—which he had to do now. After being exposed to space, the pusher's air supply was limited to his onboard oxygen and the one spare tank this pusher held.

Whoever came from Katani, it would be weeks before they arrived.

His derelict pusher floated outside, drifting away at maybe

a meter a second. It was small and fragile, torn metal and frayed wire jutting into the expanse of space. Roger's yellow helmet was visible in the cockpit.

A pretty shitty coffin, Paul thought. A pretty shitty coffin.

Paul slipped into the pilot's seat and stabilized the ship, then turned the pusher and extended a pair of its claws. Concentrating on the front end of the damaged craft, he manipulated his ship to within capture range. A few moments later he had attached and vectored his thrusters to stabilize the entire system.

He guided the pair of machines toward ZC, his own pusher now playing Goliath to the tattered remains of the other's David. Somehow, he would have to get the airlock open, a task that required the docking tube to be engaged.

As he stewed, the ZC pod loomed ahead of him like a dark skyscraper.

He scanned his display unit, punching various commands that he hoped might activate the doors remotely. But this craft was something over forty years old and hadn't had a software upgrade in probably fifteen. Nothing happened.

He sat back and thought. No ideas came.

"Damn it." He pounded on the seat's hand rest.

The station floated outside his cabin window, majestically turning against a black canvas, small pinpricks of a million worlds glittering in the background. It was images like these that had attracted him to space in the first place, slow-moving, pristine examples of physics in action.

Now this vision might be his last.

He flashed back to how Beth had hugged him before he left, each of them knowing she was worried, but neither of them saying anything about it. He thought about Heather and, finally, he thought about his dad.

Like Heather, Paul had been an only child.

He remembered how his father's eyes glistened when Paul told him he wanted to go to the Academy.

Maybe he should have stayed with his father's business, after all. Maybe, like his father before him, he should have put his kid through school selling used space junk, leaving his time in space to be the annual vacation spots, a week on

Europa, a long weekend to see the face on Mars. But that glistening in his father's eye told Paul that even his own dad understood that at the heart of the matter, the thought of leading that life made his head hurt.

"You never were one to do the expected thing," he remembered his dad saying back then, and for a minute he felt his father's presence there in the pusher with him so strongly that he thought he could smell the oily scent of space hanger that seemed to always have been around as a kid.

Paul drew a breath.

Even then he never paid attention to what was going on around him, choosing instead to spend his time hot-rigging clippers and rocket pods that lay in his father's service bays waiting for ...

An excited lump grew in Paul's throat.

There might be a way.

If he could trick the airlocks to think they were in test mode, they might open manually. He hadn't played with this type of thing for a long time, but if he didn't make it, he stood every chance of dying here, adrift in space.

Paul unbuckled from the pilot's chair and went to the airlock.

He had something less than ten minutes left in his air supply, and a good deal of work to do.

He grabbed the emergency canister and clipped it to his pack. Now he was good for a bit more than an hour.

It would have to be good enough.

He punched buttons on a panel in the back of the pusher, then pulled out an electronic package that would act as his tool set. He grabbed a utility belt complete with a pair of magnetic pliers, a hammer, and a set of ratcheted screwdrivers—all the staples of life. Stepping awkwardly into the docking chamber, Paul overrode the safety system that was designed to keep it from opening without a confirmed docking signal.

Then he pressed the purge button and waited.

The door opened.

To his left and inside the derelict pusher's frame, Roger's

yellow suit sat motionlessly in his pilot's seat, lashed to the structure like a scarecrow, one arm floating freely in zero gravity. In the distance, Goliath, the big ball of ice and ore they'd been targeting, was a dot of light that was fading in the distance. Ahead of him, the ZC pod spun silently in space, a thick column of metal and technology, lights burning inside like beacons of home, the surface rounded, but marked with electronic boxes, solar panels, and hard tubing.

He took another calming breath, then connected a tether.

"If you get me out of this one, God," Paul said, but then he didn't know how to end it, so he just let it sit.

He examined the ZC's airlock.

It was a system that consisted of a dozen or so subsystems, including pressure sensors at the door's edge and a servo controller that operated the door.

Then he jumped again, flying through vacuum toward the airlock doors.

The impact was like catching the entire station with his body.

He cradled it, holding on to an abutted ridge and a metal casing to make sure he didn't rebound into space, then crawled over the surface of the station like an oversized tarantula, checking every piece of equipment he could get his eyes on. He breathed more rapidly than he would have liked, and sweat soon soaked the first layer of his undergarments, making it sticky against his body.

Arriving at the airlock, he slipped the service control electronics chip into an open socket, and keyed in a password to deactivate the door's security system. Once in, he could toggle the test mode, and theoretically get the door to open.

A red light flashed, and the message display read, "Invalid mode of operation."

He cursed and keyed in another string of commands, a backdoor he knew worked with several older systems.

Nothing.

He closed his eyes and tried to run through the system diagram as he recalled it.

If he understood the servo mechanism's internal design, he could create a series of shorts that would break a feedback loop and command the door open. Paul knew where every wire in the area near him ran, and generally what it was for. But he had no idea how the servo's guts were strung, and without this knowledge, the chances of getting the door to open were essentially fifty-fifty. Short it the right way, the doors open, short it the wrong way, and ...

The oxygen register dropped.

His heart beat faster.

A glance at his timer said he would be dead in less than ten minutes.

First, he had to break the security system's control so he could talk with the door's servos directly. He scurried over to the door's security system and yanked power lines from its side. It took several good pulls, and by the time he was done Paul was breathing hard, using oxygen.

He crawled toward the servo box and ran a gloved finger down a thin copper conduit of bundled wires that ran to the servo.

Using pliers, he peeled back the coating until a twisted cable of green and black wire sat before him. He smelled his own fear. His breathing sounded ragged.

He needed to find the reference wire.

The door servo used a standard control algorithm, using a reference as a target to decide how to drive. When it was commanded to a voltage greater than zero, the servo would try to match that reference, driving the circuit that powered the door to activate. Same thing when it was supposed to close.

If he shorted the reference to power, it should drive the mechanism.

He gripped the pliers and picked at the wires.

There were easily fifty bundles in the conduit.

Which was the right reference?

His breathing grew labored as he peeled back the coating to follow the bundles until they got to the airlock servos. There. Those wires.

Working with fine wires while wearing space gloves was

nearly impossible, so he used pointed pliers to do most of the work, which meant he had to rip the damned wires from the connectors rather than just snip them. Still, his hands shook, and he had difficulty scuffing up the coating on a power cable. The pliers slipped from his hand, but their magnetism made them fall toward ZC's metallic surface.

His heart drummed as he retrieved the tool. The smell of his own sweat was everywhere, the wetness of his exhalation clung to his face.

Only as he breathed again did he note that his oxygen meter read zero.

He was living off the oxygen in his suit. Looking at the wiring, it was now or never. Fifty-fifty.

He grabbed a wire and pulled.

The connector gave with a yank.

Paul exhaled firmly.

As he clung to the side of the ship, he felt movement—a vibration that came through his knees and his hands. He looked down at the airlock.

It was opening.

He breathed in slowly, trying to conserve air, knowing now that even if he made it to the ZC pod, he may not have enough oxygen to pressurize the chamber in time for him to live.

Tears blurred his eyesight as he crawled to the opening.

His oxygen-starved muscles were now too weak to move properly, but he managed to loop an arm through the handhold.

His mind froze. His entire body cried out for something to breathe.

He put everything he could into another push, and suddenly found himself in the airlock itself, blinking hard against the harsh light. He pounded his hand against the pad that would engage the air lock, but missed, and had to pound again.

Behind him, the door slowly slid shut.

It was too late, though, Paul thought as he choked on air without enough oxygen. He wasn't going to make it. He wasn't going to make it.

He fell to the floor.

Cold fear crawled over his skin.

This is what it's like to die, he thought.

Beth's image came to him like a ghost of retribution.

He saw Heather.

He had been selfish in his life.

Paul Edward Daniels had left his father for the Academy, and his family for the vacuum of space. When he died, he would leave behind a wife and a daughter who would be looking for him to arrive at a party he would never see.

As Paul lost consciousness, his last act was to crack the seal on his suit's containment system.

The air lock door closed behind him.

Bugs

appeared in *Boundary Shock Quarterly*
Homo Futuris (Spring 2020) - #10

*I remember a bit by Richard Feynman—I
think from way back in the 1950s or 1960s—in
which he's talking about nanotechnology,
meaning machines the size of a couple
molecules, and how it was going to change the
world someday. I don't know if he was the first
to make such suggestions, though I suppose he
wasn't. Maybe I should Google it.*

*What I can say for sure is this was the first
time I'd been exposed to the idea. I recall being
equal parts excited and creeped out at the idea
of what these things might do inside your
body. These were the days of* Fantastic Voyage,
*after all, and since I was a young boy at the
time, being "creeped out" meant saying "oh,
cool!" and wondering what that might feel
like.*

*Run times forward a bit, and I'm doing my
own bit of science fiction work, and next thing
you know this guy John McDonald is lying in
a hospital bed, gasping for life. What follows is
a story of life, love, desperation, and, I
suppose as is inevitable, change.*

John McDonald gasped for a breath that would not come,
and in that moment understood the full definition of panic.
It was the rock inside his chest and an acid taste of fear in his

mouth. It was praying for another heartbeat. Just one.

The monitor chirped. He felt a beat. Then another.

He drew a pearl diver's breath.

Carol gripped his hand with viselike intensity, her gray-streaked hair pulled back, her face the color of hospital sheets.

"Are you okay?"

He nodded.

A distant clock marked time with audible clicks. An oxygen tube pressed uncomfortably across his upper lip.

Carol sat back in the chair she had pulled to the edge of his bed. She was the one who had kept him alive this long. She had taken control from the moment Dr. Caulder diagnosed severe cardiomyopathy—heart disease. John made the transplant list six months ago—a good first step, but eventually meaningless since there were too many patients and not enough hearts. Carol changed their diet, made him take his medicine, and mandated exercise. Never once had he seen her pessimistic side. But now her face was washed-out and faded like a character in an old Sunday afternoon movie.

"I want you to know something," he said.

"I know, John," she replied calmly. Her thumb rubbed against the back of his hand. "I know."

Another ball of cement formed in his chest. No air. Five seconds. Ten. Fifteen. Sweat lined his forehead. His thoughts ran with white noise.

Finally. A heartbeat. *Sweet mercy*. A breath.

Carol's grip shook. They stared at each other, both understanding.

"Do you love me?" he asked their rote question.

"Forever and ever," she gave the standard reply. "Forever and ever."

The door burst open.

Dr. Caulder blew into the room, the tail of his lab coat flailing in his wake. His eyes were wide behind bifocals, his thin cheeks ruddy. Wisps of hair stuck awkwardly from the sides of his head.

"We've got approval, John."

Carol gasped. Her fingertips drew to her lips, and her gaze flushed with longing that was almost painful to see.

Nurses bustled, prepping the room.

Dr. Caulder kept talking, but John could scarcely follow along. The government needed authorization. *Would he sign a waiver?* Of course, Jesus Christ, of course. His hospital gown disappeared. A nurse sprayed his chest with shaving creme. Carol's beautiful face filled his view, tears streaming down lined cheeks. She said something long and drawn out, but all John heard was "I love you." Then he was gone. Preparations continued as they rolled. IV bottles hung from steel rods. An elevator door closed. A needle pricked his arm.

Bugs, he thought. They're going to use the bugs.

Then he was asleep.

Morphine hazed his thoughts, but John felt the bugs the moment he woke up. A nurse appeared in a blue halo. She jotted a note, and punched buttons on an IV stand. The clipboard clattered against the metal rim of his bed.

His first lucid memory was the familiar chirp of a heart monitor. He smelled something bitter and felt the sensation of blankets pressing him to the bed. Where the hell was he?

John opened his eyes.

The lighting was low and gray. The ceiling tiles had patterns of holes running through them. A plastic basin sat on a rolling tray—mauve. The wall on one side was just a white curtain pulled shut. A window opened on the other side, the roof outside flat and covered with pebbles that made it look like an artificial beach.

Footsteps came from the hall.

"Good evening, Mr. McDonald," a man said as he pulled back the curtain. It was a nurse, male.

"What time is it?"

"Just past lunch." The nurse pulled the tablet from its clip on the bed rail. He was young, maybe late twenties. His hair was short and parted in the middle. Razor stubble

covered his jaw in what John understood was fashionable
these days.

"When did I go under?"

The nurse put his hand on John's forehead. "Still a little
dopey, eh?"

John read the nurse's name tag. Mark Anderson.

Anderson's breath smelled of peppermint.

"Your surgery was just past nine last night. We've kept
you sedated to make sure the devices had time to take hold.
You're coming along fine, though."

The devices. Suddenly his chest itched. He put his hand
to his chest.

"No bandages?"

"Your process was administered via hypo, Mr.
McDonald—six deep cavity shots at various angles." The
nurse pressed an instrument against John's neck.

John raised his gown. Yes, his chest was smooth, but
marked with yellow bruises.

"Why shave me, then?"

"Gotta keep the barbers employed." Nurse Anderson
smiled at his own joke. "Actually, we do that so if something
goes wrong we're prepped for emergency surgery."

John scratched his chest.

The bugs tiny machines that performed tiny jobs, each
worked together to create a whole. No different from a
pacemaker, as the promo said. But they felt like spiders
crawling around in there, their prickly legs wriggling and
spinning webs in the dark corners of his body. They moved
together, spawning, and growing, releasing their offspring to
spawn again.

He shuddered.

"Are you all right?"

"Yeah. It's just, well, I feel them in there."

"Phantom bugs." The nurse scribbled something on the
clipboard. "What does it feel like?"

"Like I got a damned ant farm in my chest. What do you
mean, phantom bugs?"

Nurse Anderson's pen didn't stop. "Some of the earliest
patients of this procedure reported the sensation of

movement inside them. No one really knows what causes them."

John and Carol had read a lot about the bugs back when Dr. Caulder first presented the idea. The *devices*, as Caulder called them, had been successful on rats and dogs. But three of the first ten humans subjected to the procedure had died within a week, and the AMA and FDA put a stop to the trial. Despite this, every biotech company in the world saw nanosurgery as the next gold mine. Competition was fierce. Approval in John's case was a major feather in Caulder's cap.

The nurse finished his notes.

"The devices are not programmed to interface with the nervous system, meaning you shouldn't feel anything, so we think it's phantom pain—like when someone loses his leg and says he feels his foot."

John put his lips together.

"Do you want the curtains closed?" the nurse said.

"No."

"Have a good day, then," Anderson said as he left.

John tried to ignore the itching. Phantom or not, the bugs gave him the creeps.

Footsteps came down the hall, and Carol entered. She was short and thin, with the same wiry grace she had carried since the day he met her. "There you are," she said.

For the first time John thought he might actually live.

"Good morning," Dr. Caulder said as he breezed into the room. "How are we doing today?"

Five interns, and a young woman carrying a palm-sized recorder followed him—a reporter, John realized. Great.

He ran his hand through his matted hair and looked at Carol, who was sitting in a chair in the corner of the room reading a magazine.

"*We* are doing fine," John finally grumbled.

Caulder grinned as he checked the IV drip and glanced at a digital readout displaying nanoactivity inside John's body. The doctor's hair was gelled, and if John didn't know better Caulder looked like he was wearing a touch of makeup.

John scratched his chest and gave a sideways glance at

the reporter. He wanted to talk to Caulder about the bugs.

"Do we have to have the camera?" he said.

Caulder grinned. "You better get used to it, John. You'll be doing *Late Night* before you know it."

"What do you mean?"

"You're all over the news, honey," Carol answered.

"That's right," Caulder said. "Every wire on the planet is buzzing about us."

"Great," he said as he looked at the camera."

Caulder scanned John's chemistry chart.

"I still feel the bugs," John blurted.

"Ah." Caulder turned to the interns. "Mr. McDonald has complained about sensations of nanoactivity inside his chest. Does anyone know what our current thinking as to what might be causing this?"

A thin kid with pimpled skin raised a hand.

Caulder pointed to the intern. "Mr. Simpson?"

"The latest proposal is that the patient is susceptible to heat released by the bug's activity."

"That's right. Though, I prefer to use the term *devices*."

The interns chuckled. The camera panned.

"We've injected several classes of devices into the patient," the doctor continued. "Rover units to protect our protein programs from the patient's immune system, Cleansers to rid the bloodstream of fatty deposits and other clogging agents, and, of course, the Medidocs—units coded to search out damaged heart tissue. Once these devices find the damaged area, they latch on. As more and more units find homes, they build a surface—almost, to use an unfortunate analogy, like a colony of ants builds a bridge."

He gave John a familiar pat on the kneecap.

"These are all machines, and machines get warm as they work."

"Hmm," John replied. It didn't feel like heat to him, but the reporter put the lens in his face and suddenly he felt like a bumbling idiot.

"Looks like you're doing great," Dr. Caulder said.

"Yeah, I feel good." And he did. He was breathing easy, and his heart seemed fine. "They've got me up and walking already."

Caulder gave him the million-dollar smile. "You'll be going home tomorrow."

"Isn't it a little early?" Carol replied.

"No reason to keep him. I want to see him every day, so we can change out his programming proteins. But the Medidocs are stable. I don't see any reason he can't go home."

John scratched his chest again. "Wonder if I'll set off airport metal detectors."

The interns laughed, and the reporter drew in for another close-up.

He woke from a nap to find his room full of people wearing lab smocks and green scrubs.

"Surprise!" a short, blonde woman at the side of his bed said with a smile. She held a cupcake with a lit candle.

"What is this?" John mumbled.

"Sorry to wake you. We're from the device lab, and we just wanted to wish you a good send-off tomorrow. I'm Sally." She shook his hand.

"Thank you," he said, accepting the cupcake.

"It's fat-free. Sorry."

He smiled and blew out the candle. They sang him "Happy Second Birthday." The cupcake was dry, but good. They each shook his hand, and wished him good luck. He thanked them each, making sure to call them each by their names—John was good at names and faces—you had to be to survive in the insurance business—and it seemed to make them each even happier.

Sally was the last to leave. "Sorry we couldn't take more time, John. But we've got a thousand things to do."

"I understand," John said. "Be sure to thank everyone for the nanobash."

She chuckled and gave John a radiant smile. "Nanobash. The gang will love it."

Before releasing him, Dr. Caulder asked John to participate in a press conference. "It's a tremendous photo op, John. I really want people to see how beneficial this procedure is. Think of the folks on the transplant list."

John was happy to agree. "I wouldn't be here without you, Doc. So if you want me to do the hokey-pokey on my way out of here, I'm your man."

Caulder laughed.

A shower and fresh clothes made him feel truly human.

Andrea Yan, a Medicorp public relations specialist, spent two hours going over questions and answers with him and Carol. Finally, it was time to leave. Dr. Caulder walked on John's left side, Carol on his right. The hospital administrator and Ms. Yan followed closely behind.

"I feel like I'm heading for the electric chair," John quipped.

"Just be ready for the questions," Caulder said.

John gave him a sideways glance. The doctor was nervous.

"How bad can it be?" he said.

Then a wave of heat hit him like a glass wall, and he saw lights, and people, and microphones that grew like metallic mushroom from every direction. Voices called from the crowd en masse.

"How are you feeling, Mr. McDonald?"

"Why did you agree to the procedure?"

"Hey, John, look this way!"

"Show us your scar!"

John put on his forced smile and nodded and held Carol close by him like Ms. Yan had coached him to.

A makeshift stage stood in front of a deep blue backdrop with the AMA emblem and the Medicorp logo pasted on it, the hospital's seal was embedded in the podium.

The media questioned Medicorp's president, who made several references to regulations and "...the new trillion-dollar market that Medicorp stands poised to be the first to leap into." Then Dr. Caulder discussed the procedure. Finally came John's turn.

The questions were a blur. *"How does it feel to be the first real robot?"* "Huh?" *"When did you first know you were sick?"* "Four or five years ago." *"Do you think you should be dead now?"* "I couldn't say, but it looked pretty bad for a while. I'm pleased that the FDA approved the procedure." Humble nods from the Medicorp staff.

"Do you get any good radio stations in there?"

Laughs from the crowd.

"Are you from the <u>Enquirer?</u>" he replied.

Thunderous laughter.

John looked at Ms. Yan. She gave only a glimmer of a smile as if to say, *I told you that line would work.*

Dr. Caulder finally stepped back onto the stage. "I'm sure you'll have ample opportunity to talk to John over the next few days. But I think it's time we let him get some rest."

Ten minutes later they were in the car. "I didn't think that would ever end," he said. Carol smiled, put the car in gear, and drove onto the interstate. John scratched his chest, feeling the bugs for the first time since the interview had started.

A television van from Channel 5 was parked across the street when they pulled in the driveway. The door slid open and a woman and a man stepped out. The woman had dark hair and lipstick, and wore a bright red blazer. Her perfume knocked him over from across the driveway.

"Welcome home, John," she said, holding a microphone. "Can we have a quick word?"

"I don't really want—"

"Hit us, Kenard."

The man pointed a camera at them. The light flared. John raised his hand to shield his eyes.

"This is Kris Cordy with Five Alive, and I'm here with nanosurgery patient John McDonald. Hi, John."

"Uh, hi."

"Can you tell us about the procedure?"

"Well, I, uh." He felt like a fool under the glare of the lights. Then the morning's training kicked in. "Dr. Caulder and the Medicorp people presented my case to various government agencies ..."

Five minutes later, Carol dragged him into the house. By then, two more television crews had arrived, and a helicopter from Channel 12 circled above them.

The phone was ringing when they walked in the door.

"Hello," Carol answered. "May I ask who is calling? ... Mr. McDonald is on doctor's orders to rest ... No, ma'am, I don't know who his representation is ... No ... No ... Thank you, but I'm not going to answer that ... Thank you. Good-bye."

She hung up quickly.

"My God, John. That was the Davis Agency. They want to talk about handling your PR."

He laughed.

Carol dialed their messaging service. "We've got ninety-eight messages, John."

"Christ."

He sat down and scratched his chest. The bugs were still in there, scratching and clawing as if they wanted out, and for the life of him it seemed like everyone else in the world was on the outside, scratching to get in.

The next day, John was sitting in the kitchen.

The remnants of his lunch littered a small plate. It had been, perhaps, the finest turkey sandwich he had ever eaten. He put the paper down and looked out the bay window. The car was in the garage. Bright sunlight fell on the white driveway.

Carol was down with the laundry.

He sat there, alone for the first time since his surgery, looking out over his back yard, and thinking about his life.

John had sent three kids to college selling insurance, put up swing sets and mowed grass, and PTA meetings whenever Carol dragged him along. He taught the kids to drive, and watched as they went on their first dates. And he had shared it all with the woman of his dreams. He had planned to retire in another four or five years. That would be his time with Carol.

Their time.

John's throat twisted. There were so many things they had left to do. He had honestly thought he was going to die. He had almost missed it all. He had almost ruined it for both of them. Now, though, he was alive and in the quiet of his own home, and he could not ever remember feeling as good as he felt at this precise moment in time. Everything was so vivid, so vital.

He suddenly wanted to be outside.

He wanted to walk, to feel the sun on his arms as they swung freely with his stride. He wanted to feel asphalt pass below his feet.

John picked his pill from the table, slipped it into his mouth, and swallowed it with the last of his milk. It was his programming pill—a time released vial of proteins that gave the bugs their marching orders. Caulder called it a PDB— protein data bus—a series of pills that fed the machines one function at a time.

The full program would complete in three weeks.

Then he would be free again.

He inhaled the aroma of wild onion amid the lingering scents of the grass outside, then stood up and rinsed the plate. Before he knew it he had his favorite floppy hat on his head and was heading toward the door.

"Where do you think you're going?"

John stopped with his hand on the doorknob.

Carol, having just returned from the basement, was leaning against the kitchen counter, arms folded across her chest.

"Just for a little walk."

"Are you trying to kill yourself, John?"

"I feel fine."

"You've only been home a day."

"I was just going down the road a bit."

"Nothing strenuous for two weeks, remember? You've already been out twice today."

He pulled the hat from his head and shrugged. "Probably just run into another reporter, anyway." He dropped the hat on the table and turned to the television.

"Is that where that goes?" Carol asked.

John grimaced, picked the hat up, and stepped into the hallway closet to put it on the top shelf.

"Seriously, John, what are you trying to do?"

"You know you're cute when you're angry, honey?" he

said as tried to engulf her in a hug.

Carol pushed away.

"Seriously, John. Be careful, okay? When you were in the hospital I thought ... well, you know what I thought. But now it's like someone hit a magic switch, and I've got you back like you're all good as new and ... I don't know."

He opened his arms.

This time she let him hug her. She felt good, her cheek buried in the fleshy part of his shoulder.

"I can't stand the idea of losing you, John."

"It's okay, now," he said, stroking the graying strands of her hair. He remembered when it was long and black. "I feel strong, honey, like I could run a marathon and not break a sweat. We're going to be together for a long time."

Carol pulled back. "I'm glad. Really, I am. Just take it easy for a while." She cocked her head toward a pile of notes on the counter by the phone. "Maybe spend some time digging through your calls."

He grumbled. Agents, talk show hosts, national news anchors—Caulder hadn't been joking. "I'm not in the mood."

"You've got to handle them sometime."

"Yeah, I know. Just not today."

The telephone rang. They chuckled at each other.

"Let the service get it," John said.

Carol nodded, then went to pull weeds from her flowerbeds.

John walked into the living room and looked at the TV. He didn't think he could stomach another game show. He picked up a book from the stand beside the couch. *The Old Man and the Sea.* It had been a long time since he had been able to just sit and read. Just his luck—now that he had the time, he was too restless to concentrate.

The phone rang again. He hung his head.

It was going to be a long couple of weeks.

He sat down and started to read.

"Dinner!" Carol called.

John looked up, surprised at the time.

The smell of garlic and fresh broccoli came from the

kitchen. Suddenly he was hungry.

Books were piled on the table beside his recliner. He frowned. Not only had he made it through *The Old Man and the Sea*, but he had read a pair of Ken Follet novels and was just finishing Stephen Hawking's *A Brief History of Time*. In the past he had read Hawking's book because it made him feel more intelligent to think about things like relativity and time, even though he never understood it all. He would read it like it was liqueur, scanning short passages and relishing the possibilities locked in its pages. This time, though, he found himself understanding Hawking's words clearly. Now he understood exactly what the space-time continuum meant.

He scratched the back of his neck.

"Are you coming?" Carol called.

"Yeah." He put the book down atop a Larry McMurtry title. Jesus. He had read *Lonesome Dove*, too.

He woke up the next morning with a hard-on—a big-time, straight-ahead, rip-roaring boner so hard it hurt.

Lines of sunlight fell across the bed, and muffled morning sounds of birds filtered through the room.

Carol was curled with her back to him.

He admired the teepee he made under the comforter. Christ. What should he do? He considered waiting it out then getting up, but that idea lasted only as long as it took to put his hand down and touch himself. His imagination kicked in, and he thought of himself atop Carol and her telling him how she felt. The idea of her legs wrapped around him was unbearable.

He rolled over and put his hand on her hip.

When she didn't react, he slid closer and pressed against her. She stirred a bit. He kissed the back of her neck. Soon she was more awake than she had been in a very long time.

The sensation in his chest returned while he was in the shower, but John no longer cared. It was great to be alive, and if the occasional tingle of bugs was his price, then by God, it was one he was willing to pay.

Still, they seemed to be lower today, twisting around in the area of his stomach and intestines. His kidneys itched while he was shaving. His skin tingled. Ideas raced through his head so fast he felt like it might explode.

When he rubbed himself dry he got another erection.

Christ, it was great to be alive.

The smell of eggs and toast hung in the air as he stepped into the kitchen.

"Perfect timing," Carol said over her shoulder.

She wore a pair of wrinkled sweats and one of his T-shirts. She smeared butter on a piece of toast.

"What's this?"

"It's called breakfast."

"I didn't think we did big breakfast anymore."

She handed him a plate with an omelet. Her grin was mischievous. "I thought you deserved something special."

John ground pepper over his omelet.

Another programming pill sat beside his napkin. A pile of newspapers sat on the table. A tabloid headline proclaimed he was discovered communicating to his homeland in outer space.

"Look, honey, I'm a Martian."

She smirked as she sat beside him. "I thought you would like that one."

He took a bite, tasting cheese and mushroom and onion in perfect balance. The toast was wheat, crisp and fresh, with butter and a perfectly thin layer of raspberry jam.

"This is the best omelet I've ever tasted."

"I bet you say that to all the girls."

He laughed. "I think I'm going to call *The Late Show*."

"I thought you didn't want to do that kind of thing."

"You only go around once, you know?" he said with a shrug. "Besides, it would be nice to see California, don't you think? We could rent a car and drive back. Maybe stop at the Grand Canyon on the way. Or Vegas."

"Feeling lucky?"

He raised a leering eyebrow.

"We need to start planning these things," he said. "We

need to start living again."

"Are you okay?" she said, staring at him.

"Yeah," he said, not knowing exactly what to say next. "I think I'm okay. It's like I'm a kid again."

"I'd second that," she replied.

"I'm serious. I feel great. Things taste better, they sound better. It's like ... I don't know what it's like."

"Maybe you should talk to Dr. Caulder this afternoon."

He nodded, and took another bite of toast. Butter, jam, robust and full of citric life—gloriously sweet and smooth. It was enough to make a grown man cry.

"Sorry to keep you waiting," Dr. Caulder said as he stepped into his office. John and Carol had been there for forty-five minutes. The parade of nurses, technicians, needles, protein programmers, CAT scans, and X-rays had long since served to kill whatever patience they may have had.

"Is he okay?" Carol said.

"His nanoactivity is abnormally high."

"What does that—"

The doctor held up his hand to stop Carol's question. "We tested the devices in your blood sample, John, and discovered the interface has grown." He glanced at Carol. "What that means is—"

"My bugs are changing the way they communicate."

"Yes," Caulder said. "They're still using the central protein bus we designed for them, so they get our commands. But additional communication paths have spontaneously grown."

The doctor looked at John with an expectant expression.

"You've found new bugs, haven't you? Ones you never injected."

The doctor nodded. "How did you guess?"

"I spent this morning reading your material about how the devices are programmed. Different bugs for different types of cells, one design for smooth muscle, another for striated—one bug for neural work, another for skeletal cells. The Internet has better descriptions than your pamphlets, by the way. Anyway, it isn't much of a leap to guess that if the bugs are making new communications interfaces, they're likely making new systems."

"You're right," the doctor said.

Carol's gaze flashed between Caulder and her husband. She clenched her fists, and her jaw worked in that way she had when she was truly angry. "What the hell are you talking about?"

John turned to face his wife. "The bugs are doing things they weren't supposed to, and they've developed a way to make more of themselves."

"Maybe," Caulder said. "We don't know much, yet. Give the techs a couple days. In the meantime, the scans show John's heart is totally enclosed and is being supported by the devices just as planned. So we're moving into the final repair stage with the programming proteins."

"Where else are they?" John said.

"You've got a mechmass at the base of your medulla oblongata, and a few in your kidneys, spleen, several joints. But we don't see any damage at this point so there's no reason to panic. I've got the lab work on a blocking protein— essentially a big mask that should stop the devices from being able to read anything we don't feed them directly."

"So it won't shut them off, but they'll be blind to any new commands," John said.

"That's right."

"They'll be in the next set of pills?" Carol asked.

Caulder nodded. "And we'll give John an injection now to get the new program started, and we've got a pair of oral doses prepared for this evening and tomorrow morning."

They were silent for an awkward moment.

"Well," Carol said. "I guess we wait and see."

John knew before they went to bed that he wasn't getting any sleep, and had only slipped under the covers to encourage Carol. Now it was 1:00 a.m. and he felt warm. He saw bugs in the darkened corners of his thoughts. He heard them in the recesses of his auditory canals.

The skin along his arm burned.

His fingernail caught on something when he scratched it, so he scratched more. His skin felt crusty, but he couldn't see anything in the dark. He slipped out of bed, padded to the bathroom, and closed the door before flicking on the light.

A gray disk had grown on his forearm. It was oblong and metallic like a drop of lead the approximate surface area of a dime. He rubbed it. Tiny gray fragments clung to his fingertip.

Bugs.

Thousands. Millions. Maybe trillions of bugs crawling over his skin.

He looked at his face in the mirror but saw no signs of them there. He pulled off his pajama shirt. A pinhole showed on the fleshy part of his deltoid. He stripped off his pants and found nothing, but a scrubbing sensation had started low on the right side of his groin.

His hands shook. Holy God.

He gulped air and looked in the mirror again. He had to call Dr. Caulder. He went downstairs to dial.

"Hello, you have reached the answering service of Dr. Peter Caulder ..." John punched the "1" without waiting for the automatic menu. The phone rang five times before someone answered.

He cut the operator off before she could speak. "This is John McDonald. I need to talk to Dr. Caulder immediately."

"I'm sorry, who is this, again?" the nameless woman said.

"John McDonald. Hurry."

"Oh. You're the guy with the bugs."

"Yes," he said in exasperation.

"How does it feel to be on TV?"

"Jesus fucking Christ, lady! I didn't call you at one in the goddamned morning to chat about television. Get me Caulder right now."

The phone crackled with awkward silence.

"Uh, I'll have to have him call you back."

"Fine." John squeezed the phone so tight his fingers grew white. "That's fine. He's got my number."

He put the phone down. The case was split along its length.

John glanced at his open palm.

They were in there. He could feel them working away, changing him. Standing naked in his kitchen, staring at the juxtaposition of the broken phone and the gray leaden disk on his arm, John McDonald began to hyperventilate.

The phone rang.

"Dr. Caulder?"

"What's the matter, John?"

"I don't know. I've got bugs coming out of my freaking arm."

Caulder didn't reply immediately. John's scalp tingled.

"Meet me at the hospital in an hour?" Caulder finally said.

"Yeah. An hour."

"Don't panic, okay? Everything will be fine."

"Easy for you to say," John said.

"See you there."

The phone clicked dead. The dial tone buzzed.

John slipped into the bedroom and picked out pants and shoes and a pullover sweatshirt. He debated waking Carol, but wanted to spare her the sight of bugs eating through his body. He smirked. Who was he kidding? The gray spots made his stomach sick. Down in the root of his bones he was afraid. The truth was that he didn't want his wife to see him like this.

With luck he would be back before she woke up, anyway.

So he wrote Carol a note and left her asleep.

It was 1:45 in the morning when John rolled into the lot. He parked next to a black BMW with a GeneoTech sticker affixed to the lower right corner of its windshield. He scratched his arm. GeneoTech was one of Medicorp's competitors. Perhaps he should have used them.

A security guard nodded as John headed to the elevators. The third floor smelled of cleanser. He stepped around a huge polishing machine standing sentry in the middle of the hallway. The route to Caulder's office took him by the device lab, a large room with glass-panel walls, bright lights, and chrome-coated equipment.

He glanced in as he padded through the hallway. Five techs were working, and a man in a blue sweater stood beside the tech at the far end of one workbench. They were pointing at a screen. John thought about pounding on the window and waving hello, but didn't.

Caulder was probably driving them pretty hard now.

The waiting room to the doctor's office was open.

He flipped on the light and took a seat, scanning the now familiar coffee table filled with neatly aligned copies of *NanoTimes* and *The Medical Journal of Biotech.* He closed his eyes and saw himself morphing into a gray mass of churning levers, rods, and rotors.

Jesus. Get a handle, man.

He took a deep breath, scratching his arm.

Something was wrong here, though, something out of kilter.

He felt uneasy.

The clock read 1:55—probably fifteen or twenty minutes before Caulder got here. John lifted his collar. The pinpoint on his shoulder had grown. The spot on his forearm was larger, too. He glanced to the device lab. The man in the blue sweater was still leaning over the workspace with the lab techs.

That's what had nagged him.

He had met all the techs at one point or another, but John didn't recognize this man. John stepped out of Caulder's office and pressed against the lab wall. Blue sweater was maybe thirty-five, and just beginning to show a bulge at his waist. His hair was black, trimmed short. John was positive he had never seen him before.

He strained to hear their conversation.

"The connection to the spinal column is complete," one of the techs said.

"Yeah," blue sweater replied. "And the optimizer units are working. After today's scare we'll have to pull them back a bit or Caulder will figure this out."

John knitted his eyebrows together.

"He'll be back for more masks tomorrow," the tech said. "What do you want to do?"

Blue sweater straightened and put his hands on his hips.

"Let's cool it on the optimizers for now, and work on getting the respiratory anchors in place?"

"You got it."

Blue sweater patted the tech's shoulder. "Gotta run. See you tomorrow night?"

"Sounds good."

John backed into a dark recess as the man walked down the hallway and pressed a button for the elevator. John didn't want to lose him. The elevators would take too long to arrive, so he took the stairs, two at a time, rushing downward.

The elevator chimed as he hit the ground floor.

Blue sweater waved at the guard as he left. The guard gave John a quizzical stare as he followed, but didn't say anything.

The man walked toward the car next to John's.

John's eyes fell on the GeneoTech symbol.

Holy shit. Blue Sweater man worked for GeneoTech. *Dr. Caulder didn't know what was happening because these weren't his bugs.*

Suddenly John wanted to hit this man, wanted to squash him like the cockroach he was. The asshole. The total asshole. John strode forward, than ran, his feet pounding against the asphalt, his rage pounding against his temples.

"Wha—"

The man looked up just in time to catch John's right cross. He fell against the car, then slid to the ground, blood flowing from his nose. He tried to crawl, but could barely manage to lift himself.

John kicked the car door and left a dent.

"I'm John McDonald. Unless you want to go to jail for the rest of your life, I suggest you start talking."

"What the hell are you doing?" the man said as he regained his senses.

John ripped his shirtsleeve back to his elbow, grabbed the man by the collar, lifted him up to push him against his Beamer, and shoved his forearm into the man's nose.

"What the hell is this?"

Blue Sweater focused on John's arm. "Woah!"

"What's your name?"

"Martin. Martin Sprawling."

"You work for GeneoTech."

"Yeah." The man put his fingers to his bleeding nose. "It's probably a reaction to the mask they ran today. We can fix it."

John tightened his hold of Sprawling's collar. "What's in the bugs you're giving me?"

Sprawling looked as if he were judging how much to say.

John twisted his grip, raised the man off the ground and crushed him against the car.

Sprawling winced.

"GeneoTech is out of business either way, asshole" John said.

Sprawling gave in. "There's a bunch of different ones, but the most important are neural links and triage systems."

"What the hell do they do?"

"They fix you. They find things they think can improve, then build whatever kind of bug they need to fix it."

"They're making me better?"

Sprawling nodded. "They're making you more of who you can be."

Spiders tingled in his veins.

"Christ."

He threw Sprawling to the ground and kicked another dent into the BMW's door. Sprawling tried to crawl away, but John kicked him in the ribs and pinned him against the asphalt.

"Did you actually think you could get away with this?"

He realized immediately how stupid that question was. Anyone in the insurance business knew just how far a company was willing to go when that kind of money was on the table.

"I can't believe you've got the entire Medicorp lab on your payroll."

"Just the night shift and a couple protein programmers." Martin Sprawling squirmed against John's restraint, blood trickling down his chin. "Maybe we can make a deal."

"I don't deal with dirt."

"Think about it, John. Think about it hard. I can make you into a Miracle Man. You're already probably going to live forever."

John tightened his lips, digesting that thought. "What?"

"The bugs are optimizing everything."

John stood, thinking, still absorbing. Could he live forever?

"We're both big boys here," Sprawling said. "What do you want?"

The question hung like a cloud. A gust of wind blew his hair. Streetlight reflected off the metallic lump on his forearm. The skin on his scalp tingled and he felt bugs crawling in his brain.

What if he did? What if he lived forever?

What did he want?

"I want my life back."

"I don't think it's a good idea to take the bugs out."

"I don't want you to take them out."

"I don't understand."

"Here's what you're going to do," John said.

By breakfast, the bugs had grown him a new skin, soft and smooth, pale, a nearly perfect match for his own. GeneoTech delivered the new program that afternoon while Carol was out shopping.

John was sitting at the kitchen table when she returned.

"Hi," she said without looking at him.

He watched her put grocery bags on the counter, remembering how she used to look striding over open ground.

"What's that goofy look for?"

"Do you love me?"

She stared at him. "Are you all right?"

He told her everything, explained how GeneoTech slipped foreign bugs into the mix, about his eyesight, which was so good now he no longer needed glasses. He talked about how it felt to walk without pain in his knees, about smells and sounds and the taste of butter on toast. He explained how

Caulder was going to extend the mask, but how it wasn't going to matter.

"I'm going to live a very long time," he finally said.

Carol looked at him as if she didn't know him.

"What about me?" Carol whispered. "What about us?"

John fished the vial from his pocket and put it on the table. Her gaze lingered on it.

"What about the kids."

"Maybe someday. But for now it's just you and me. No one else can know."

"What if something goes wrong?"

His stare was pleading. The refrigerator kicked on. Carol wiped away a tear. "I'm still me, Carol. I don't feel different anywhere that matters."

She bit her upper lip. "This is a lot to absorb."

"Yes, it is. Take your time." He stood to leave her alone, to give her space to think.

"Wait," she said. She picked up the vial, looked at it first, then at John.

"Do you love me?" she said.

He smiled. "Forever and ever."

She twisted the lid.

If you enjoyed these stories, find Ron's work at
http://www/typosphere.com

For more from *Boundary Shock Quarterly*, check out their
website: http://www.boundaryshockquarterly.com.

If you sign up for Ron's newsletter, you'll get a free copy of
Glamour of the God-Touched, Volume 1 of *Saga of the God-
Touched Mage.*

http://www.typosphere.com/newsletter

Acknowledgement

Blaze Ward is a fun guy to be around.

He's a writer at his core, boisterous in a quiet kind of way, able to find the right thing to say at the right time. His ability to rustle up a damned fine pan of brownies is something I suggest everyone experience at least once in their life.

He's also a guy of action. See something, do something. Hence this whole *Boundary Shock Quarterly* project— which, as far as I can tell, started on a whim and spark inside his brain and has just grown from there.

Without his request, these stories wouldn't exist. And, yeah, while I hope they've been great fun to read, I *know* they've been great fun to write.

So my thanks goes officially out to Blaze Ward for his kick-ass idea and his work in getting it all together.

Here's to a couple more years.

Boundary Shock Quarterly
Year One

- **Captain's Log (Winter 2018) – #1.**
  - *For many of us, those opening words "Captain's Log..." were our introduction to our science fiction dreams. Voyages to explore strange, new worlds, seek out new life, and boldly go. What will we find out there, when we go? What dangers will we confront? Who will survive?*

- **Tuesday After Next (Spring 2018) - #2**
  - *Not all science fiction is about galactic exploration. Right now, the future is being born as computers grow ever-more-powerful, and technology wrests control of the industrial heights from the traditional powers. After Dieselpunk and before Cyberpunk, you have the Makers and the Hackers, modern rebels hiding and striking from the shadows. Welcome to the Tuesday After Next.*

- **Grand Theft Starship (Summer 2018) - #3**
  - *The future is not always a bright and shining beacon on a hill somewhere. Crime will follow us into space and the galaxy. What will you steal, with the whole galaxy to pick from?*

- **Robots, Androids, Cyborgs, Oh My! (Fall 2018) - #4**
  - *We can make him better than he was. Or build a better one to replace him. What does it mean to be Sentient? Human? Or even alive?*

Year Two

- **Boneyard of Lost Dreams (Winter 2019) - #5**
  - *All spaceships, like all travelers, grow old and retire someplace quiet, until someone comes along. What will you find on the old derelict? Or hiding in the junkyard of forgotten starships and lost dreams?*

- **Ray Guns and Space Babes (Spring 2019) - #6**
  - *Pulp. Freshly squeezed. Throw it back to bad 30's and 40's tropes and archetypes. Lantern-jawed heroes. Femme fatales. Scantily-clad princesses. Scenery chewing villains. And Dr. Basil Exposition in a white coat.*

- **Apocalypse Descending (Summer 2019) - #7**
  - *The world is ending. Right here. Right now. How? Why? What's next?*

- **Asteroid Miners and Comet Wildcatters (Fall 2019) - #8**
  - *So it turns out Einstein was right. FTL is not possible and we are pretty much stuck here. What happens to humanity when the stars turn out to be unreachable dreams?*

Year Three

- **Alien Dreams (Winter 2020) - #9**
  - ○ *What is science fiction, if not an exploration of who we'll find when we get out there? What will they be like? Alien life. Alien viewpoints. Alien Dreams.*

- **Homo Futuris (Spring 2020) - #10**
  - ○ *Medicine is on the verge of conquering disease and aging. Of making it possible to clone ourselves and make our children super beings. Or morlocks. What will the world be like when science conquers life itself?*

- **What Might Have Been (Summer 2020) - #11**
  - ○ *Time travel stories are as old as science fiction, wandering backwards to change the past or forward like Buck Rogers trapped in that abandoned mine shaft. Perhaps you will step through a mirror darkly. How will the world change? How will you?*

- **Lawmen and Crime Fighters (Fall 2020) - #12**
  - ○ *Crime will go into space faster than law enforcement jurisdictions. What will the wild west of deep space look like, to the men and women who have to protect it?*

Year Four

- **Solarpunk (Winter 2021) - #13**
  - *Solarpunk is a movement in speculative fiction, art, fashion and activism that seeks to answer and embody the question "what does a sustainable civilization look like, and how can we get there?"*

- **Space Marines (Spring 2021) - #14**
  - *Space opera is more than just starships boldly going. It is also the grunt on the ground with the rifle, just trying to survive.*

- **Cargo Wars (Summer 2021) - #15**
  - *Traders and Merchants and Goods, Oh My!*

- **Wandering Monsters (Fall 2021) – #16**
  - *Kaiju and blobs and science gone wrong. Monsters from deep space come to destroy us all or the ones quietly hiding below as colonists and Terraformers arrive.*

About Ron Collins

Ron Collins is an Amazon best-selling Dark Fantasy author who writes across the spectrum of speculative fiction. You can find his work at all major online retailers. With his daughter, Brigid, he is also editing anthologies in the Fiction River series.

His short fiction has received a Writers of the Future prize and a CompuServe HOMer Award. His short story "The White Game" was nominated for the Short Mystery Fiction Society's 2016 Derringer Award.

He holds a degree in Mechanical Engineering, and has worked to develop avionics systems, electronics, and information technology before chucking it all to write full-time, which he now does from his home in the shadows of the Santa Catalina Mountains.

Discover other work by Ron Collins at:

Amazon.com
Kobo.com
Barnesandnoble.com
Smashwords.com
Books2Read

Follow Ron at:
http://www.typosphere.com
Twitter: @roncollins13